Dressed only in jeans, Luke stood in the darkened room at the back of the house and stared across the moonlit lawn. He could make out the hump of the small cottage sheltered by trees at the edge of the hospital grounds.

Theresa's place. No, not Theresa—Terri.

Was she tucked up asleep? He glanced at his watch. One o'clock. He'd be willing to bet she wasn't lying awake thinking about him the way he was about her.

He leaned his forearm on the wooden window frame and contemplated his reaction to her this afternoon. Surely it had to be a product of his recent upheavals: the move, travelling, worry over his father and his daughter.

But that one tiny and very public hug with Terri had evoked such a powerful memory that he'd been swept back twelve years to the last time he'd held her in his arms. To a five-minute interlude on the beach.

Luke rubbed his jaw, feeling the rasp of stubble. It had been ridiculous.

And potentially disastrous.

Born in New Zealand, **Sharon Archer** now lives in county Victoria, Australia, with her husband Glenn, one lame horse and five pensionable hens. Always an avid reader, she discovered Mills & Boon as a teenager through Lucy Walker's fabulous Outback Australia stories. Now she lives in a gorgeous bush setting, and loves the native fauna that visits regularly... Well, maybe not the possum which coughs outside the bedroom window in the middle of the night.

The move to acreage brought a keen interest in bushfire management (she runs the fireguard group in her area), as well as free time to dabble in woodwork, genealogy (her advice is...don't get her started!), horse-riding and motorcycling—as a pillion or in charge of the handlebars.

Free time turned into words on paper! And the dream to be a writer gathered momentum. With her background in a medical laboratory, what better line to write for than Mills & Boon® Medical™ Romance?

Recent titles by the same author:

MARRIAGE REUNITED: BABY ON THE WAY
SINGLE FATHER: WIFE AND MOTHER WANTED

BACHELOR DAD, GIRL NEXT DOOR

BY
SHARON ARCHER

First published in Great Britain 2010
Harlequin Mills & Boon Limited,
Eton House, 18-24 Paradise Road, Richmond, Surrey TW9 1SR

© Sharon Archer 2010

ISBN: 978 0 263 21492 5

Harlequin Mills & Boon policy is to use papers that are natural,
renewable and recyclable products and made from wood grown in
sustainable forests. The logging and manufacturing process conform
to the legal environmental regulations of the country of origin.

Printed and bound in Great Britain
by CPI Antony Rowe, Chippenham, Wiltshire

BACHELOR DAD,
GIRL NEXT DOOR

CHAPTER ONE

LUKE DANIELS ran an idle glance over the sleek silver motorcycle stopped in the lane beside him at the traffic light. Through his closed windows he could hear the throb of the powerful engine. An unexpected spark of interest fought with deep unease.

It'd been years since seeing a bike had had any sort of effect on him. How odd that it should be now, when he was back in Port Cavill to stay—at least for the year-long term of his contract.

But perhaps that was why.

Port Cavill. The scene of his first medical failure.

'Are we nearly there?' His daughter's sulky voice interrupted his dark thoughts.

'Not far, Allie.' He rolled his neck, feeling the tiredness and tension in his muscles.

'Alexis,' she corrected with all the disdain a ten-year-old could muster.

Luke stifled a sigh. He wasn't popular and there wasn't anything he could do about it.

Except get on a plane back to England.

Even the weather conspired to make things unpleasant. The earlier sunny heat had given way to oppressive humidity, which the car's air-conditioning was struggling to cope with. Glowering banks of cloud still pressed down with the threat of more rain to come.

He studied Allie's sullen profile and debated whether to point out again that they'd only be here for a year. Long enough for him to help his father get back on his feet. Long enough to seem like a lifetime in a child's eyes. Times like this he longed for Sue-Ellen's wise counsel. But his wife, Allie's mother, had been buried two years ago. So loving, so giving. And too damned young to die.

'That person on the bike's waving at you, Dad. Who is it?'

He looked in the direction of Allie's pointing finger.

'I don't know.'

The pillion passenger began pulling at the rider's shoulder until the person must have retaliated with an admonition to keep still. Catching Allie's eye, Luke smiled. 'Kind of hard to tell with that helmet on, isn't it?'

His daughter shrugged, letting him know a moment of shared humour couldn't woo her.

The lights changed and the bike pulled away sedately enough to merge into his lane ahead. Following slowly, he allowed the distance to stretch because of the wet road. The pillion passenger turned to check behind. Luke shook his head in irritation. The action would shift the weight, unbalance the bike. He felt a twinge of sympathy for the poor rider.

Movement from a side road caught his peripheral vision. A car fishtailed into the intersection.

Had the motorcyclist seen it?

Heart pounding, hands clenched on the steering-wheel, he waited for the inevitable disaster. Suddenly the rider reacted, the brake light flicked on.

'Too late,' Luke muttered. 'Counter-steer.'

A split second later, the rider obeyed his command. Relief quickly swooped into despair as the wheels skidded precariously on the slick surface.

In the time it took for rider to control the bike, graphic memories of another, less fortunate motorcycle leapt out of the past to assault him. A battered racer, twisted metal. The smell of hot tar and spilled petrol.

The smell of blood.

His cousin's moans of pain.

A line of sweat chilled Luke's upper lip as he remembered the helplessness. The hopelessness when he'd realised the extent of Kevin's injuries. Nausea rolled through his stomach.

Super-sensitised now to the progress of the bike and the actions of the cars around it, Luke could feel irrational, burning anger growing. He'd successfully suppressed the anguish for the thirteen years since the accident. Now in the blink of an instant it was all there, raw and powerful.

He wished the rider would turn off so he could stop worrying about them but they were travelling inexorably in the same direction. Slowing more, he let the distance widen, until several other cars filled the gap.

By the time he got to his turn-off, they'd disappeared.

Relief was short-lived. He turned into his parents' driveway to see the bike parked on the gravel.

Still helmeted and astride the machine, the rider seemed to be delivering a well-deserved lecture to the dismounted pillion passenger.

'That's Aunty Megan,' said Allie.

Hell! Luke clenched his jaw as a cold chill swept his body. What was his baby sister doing hooning around Port Cavill on the back of a bloody motorcycle?

'Stay here,' he ordered his daughter as he flicked his seat-belt catch off.

He stalked towards the pair at the bike, relishing the thought of tearing strips off them after the fright they'd given him.

'Luke!' Megan launched herself at him, enveloping him in an enthusiastic hug. He clamped her close, intensely thankful for her vitality and safety. Determined to make sure she stayed that way. 'We weren't expecting you until tomorrow.'

'We came straight through from the airport,' he said after a moment. Holding her away from him, he frowned. 'Your bad luck I was here to see that stunt you and your friend here pulled back in town. You think I want to spend my first day home scraping you two off the road?'

'Oh, don't you start, too.' Megan threw her hands up. 'Terri was just going off at me about it.'

'Yeah?' Luke aimed a black look at the rider. 'Maybe he'll think twice before he takes you on the bike again.'

'But Terri's—'

'In fact, let's make that official.' God, he'd been back in town for less than half an hour and he was already standing toe to toe with his sister. Part of his anger was tiredness. But most of it was fear. If he had the power to prevent it, he wasn't going to lose another member of his family.

And this was definitely within his power. 'You're grounded.'

'Honestly, Luke!' Megan planted her hands on her hips.

'Does Mum know what you're up to?'

'I'm nearly eighteen.' Her chin jutted defiance as she glared at him.

'Is that a no?'

'No, it's not a *no*. She doesn't mind if I'm with Terri.'

'She will after I've spoken to her,' he said grimly.

'But Terri's a really careful rider.'

'Too bad. I don't want to see you on the back of this bike, any bike, again.' He directed a narrow-eyed look at the rider.

Brown eyes, so dark they were nearly black, watched him. The hint of wry amusement in them had him clenching his jaw against a scathing comment.

The motorcyclist took off the padded gloves and began fiddling with the helmet strap.

Luke was reluctantly impressed that the boy was prepared to stay in the face of the conflict. 'Look, Terry, this is a family argument. You don't want to get involved, mate. All you need to know is Megan's off the social circuit until further notice. There's no point hanging around.'

'Gee. That's going to be kind of tough, Luke,' said Megan smugly. 'Since you guys are going to be working together.'

'What?' He turned on his sister. 'You mean Mum's letting you go out with one of the hospital staff?'

'One of the doctors.' The sly look she slanted him should have been a warning. 'Terri's taught me heaps.'

Luke felt his anger crank up several notches.

'That's a recommendation I can do without,' said a husky feminine voice beside him.

The tirade he'd been about to unleash faltered on his tongue.

The rider slipped off the helmet and balanced it on the handlebars. Long black hair slithered over the protective leather jacket as the woman dismounted and turned to face him.

'Hello, Luke. Long time, no see.'

'Terri?' He gaped, his stunned brain struggling to put the name together with the evidence before his eyes. 'Theresa O'Connor.'

'Close enough. How are you?' She held out a hand and he stared at it stupidly for a long moment.

'Bloody hell. Theresa O'Connor.' He used her hand to tug her into a hug. It was quick, lasting only a second. Meant to be social, asexual. Nothing to precipitate the volcanic heat that swept through him.

He swallowed and set her away at arm's length.

Her continued stillness, her composure, unsettled him out of all proportion. Especially the small smile curving her lips.

Suddenly, Luke remembered the last time he'd seen her. On the moonlit beach at the bottom of the hospital grounds. Could it really have been twelve years ago? The memory felt too intense. She hadn't been so calm then. Though neither had he. He'd just kissed her.

He focussed on her mouth. Those lovely full lips had been soft and hesitant then eager, even demanding, beneath his.

Until he'd pushed her away.

He blinked and dragged his gaze back to hers. She stepped away, unruffled by their contact except for a tell-tale wariness in her eyes. 'It's Terri Mitchell these days.'

'Yes, of course.' He had so many questions but he felt oddly tongue-tied. His body's unexpected response to her, that hot fizz of recognition, left him unbalanced.

His memory tripped in with details supplied over the years by his mother and Theresa's brother, Ryan. Theresa was widowed, her husband killed when they'd been working with an aid organisation in Africa. An explosion. She'd been injured, too.

He cleared his throat before speaking into the lengthening silence. 'Theresa, I was sorry to—'

'No harm done.' She cut him off quickly, a tiny flare of dismay in her dark chocolate eyes. The smile on her lips looked stiff, unnatural and he realised her misunderstanding had been deliberate. Theresa didn't want to hear his words of condolence.

She glanced behind him, her smile warming. 'You must be Alexis. Your grandmother's told me all about you.'

'Alexis, this is an old friend of the family.' Luke drew his daughter forward, leaving his arm across her shoulders as he made the introductions. He was pleasantly surprised when she leaned into his side instead of shrugging him off.

She glowed under Theresa's attention. Gone was the surly, uncooperative child of mere minutes ago.

Theresa's serene surface was so firmly in place, the moment of panic seemed as though it was a figment of his imagination. Still, there was something…a hint of sadness shadowing her eyes and smile. With her attention on Allie, he could see it much more clearly.

After a few minutes, Theresa said, 'I'll leave you all to catch up properly.'

'Mum said for you to come to tea tonight, Terri,' Megan said.

'Oh. Thank your mum for me, Megan, but I have some paperwork to do before tomorrow. See you later, Alexis.' Her friendly smile faded as she raised her eyes to his. 'Luke.'

He wondered if her refusal of the dinner invitation was because of his arrival or if the paperwork excuse was genuine.

She mounted the bike, slid the helmet over her luxurious hair. Her long slender fingers worked quickly to buckle the strap beneath her chin before she reached out to turn the key in the ignition. The machine throbbed to life.

Much to Luke's surprise, she rode down the extended driveway beside his parents' house.

'So, I guess that means I can keep riding with Terri,' Megan said.

He sent her a noncommittal look. 'We'll see.'

'Luke!'

He grinned at her wailed protest and slid his question in casually. 'Is Theresa staying in the beach cottage?'

'Terri. She prefers Terri.'

'Terri, then.' He raised an eyebrow.

'Uh-huh. She's been renting it since she came back.'

He wondered why his mother hadn't told him when she'd been giving him updates on the latest Port Cavill gossip.

'And that was, what, six months ago?'

'About.' Megan shrugged.

'It's a hovel.'

'That's when *you* used to live there, Luke. Terri's done it up.'

'Really.' Perhaps he might find an opportunity to wander down for a visit, see how his old bachelor pad had scrubbed up. Learn more about the intriguing tenant...

Or perhaps not.

He was here for a year and would have his hands full with the hospital, his father and Allie. Meeting Terri again like this had tipped him out of kilter, that was all. He was tired, maybe even a little jet-lagged. Not thinking straight.

The last thing he needed was to complicate his life. Especially with someone who must thrive on excitement if the bike and her previous job were anything to judge by.

Seeing her had plunged him into an odd time warp where he relived their kiss on the beach. Could it really have been twelve years ago? He hadn't treated her particularly well that night, rejecting her soft sympathy, allowing his bitterness and guilt over his cousin's death to colour the things he'd said.

Still, she was obviously made of stern stuff. She'd gone on to do her medical training.

He'd had no interest in women during the two and a half years since Sue-Ellen's death. How damned inconvenient that the sexual spark missing in his life since then should choose to wake up now.

In Port Cavill. Of all places.

With a colleague. Someone he needed to work with for the next year. The time and place and person couldn't be worse.

Terri parked the bike beside the cottage, thankful to have made the short journey without disgracing herself by stalling or missing a gear. Or dropping the bike. She huffed out a long breath before putting down the stand and dismounting on shaky legs.

Luke was back.

Helmet tucked under one arm, she collected her handbag from the top box. She'd known he was coming home, of course. Most of the Daniels family had been in a happy buzz of anticipation for the last couple of weeks.

Except for Will Daniels. He'd been upset that, despite his recommendation, the board had appointed Luke to the position of hospital director. A position she'd been acting in since Will's myocardial infarct. Worse was that the notification had only come yesterday.

Terri had stifled her disappointment so she could reassure her convalescing boss that it didn't matter.

But it *did* matter. She'd been relishing the responsibility. It was good for her, challenging, restoring her sense of self. Giving her a much-needed focus for her shattered life.

She sighed. Perhaps even more distressing was her ridiculous fluttery reaction to Luke. How long had it been since she'd felt that disturbing feminine awareness of a man? Such lightness had had no place in her life for so many years. To have it now felt wrong, frivolous.

She crossed to the door and let herself into the cottage. Her hand lingered on her helmet for a moment after she'd placed it on the hall-stand. When Luke had confronted her and Megan, the temptation to stay inside the fibreglass dome and hide behind the smoky Perspex visor had been overwhelming. Behaviour much more in keeping with the starry-eyed teenager she'd been last time they'd met.

Why couldn't she have been caught on the ward, performing some marvellously complex medical procedure? Saving lives, saving the world, she mocked herself silently. That would have been too perfect.

She slipped off her jacket and hung it on the peg by the door. Naturally, Luke *had* to arrive a day early, catch her kitted out in motorcycle leathers and then mistake her for Megan's boyfriend.

Still, she thought she'd handled the meeting with reasonable aplomb. Thanks to the helmet, she'd had a chance to gather her wits a little before revealing herself. If anything, it had been Luke who'd been nonplussed. Embarrassed by his mistake probably.

He'd hugged her. Spontaneously. She wrapped her arms around her body, remembering the feel of his firm hold, his torso pressed to hers for those long seconds. Not that it meant anything. The Daniels family was naturally, delightfully, demonstrative.

Unlike the O'Connors.

Unlike the Mitchells. Her husband's family had saved their affections for their causes. And those they'd pursued with dedication and passion. No sacrifice too great. She grimaced, chiding herself for her disloyalty. Hating the bitterness of her thoughts.

In the kitchen, she filled the kettle. While she waited for the water to boil, she scanned the scrubby trees that bordered the back yard. The sandy path to the beach was well hidden. Astounding that she'd had the temerity to follow Luke down the track all those years ago. What a crush she'd had on him, poor sad child that she'd been.

She shook her head then spooned a scant teaspoon of coffee into a mug.

That was the past. This was now and she wasn't an angst-ridden teenager any more.

She'd been married…and widowed. The explosion that killed her husband had ripped her life apart. She'd come to Port Cavill to give herself a chance to recover, to regroup. She'd come here for peace. Nothing more.

As she contemplated the future, she pursed her lips.

Stepping into the role of director had given her a new sense of purpose. She'd been doing a damned good job even if the paperwork part of the job wasn't her forte.

Now she had to step aside.

Gracefully.

Luke's return was difficult on so many levels. Peace would be in short supply while he was around.

She sighed. At least, their first meeting was over now. Next time she encountered him, she'd be working for him.

CHAPTER TWO

DRESSED only in jeans, Luke stood in the darkened room at the back of the house and stared moodily across the moonlit lawn. He could make out the hump of the small cottage sheltered by trees at the edge of the lawn.

Theresa's place. No, not Theresa—Terri.

Was she tucked up, asleep? He glanced at his watch. Half past one in the morning. He'd be willing to bet she wasn't lying awake thinking about him, the way he was about her.

He leaned his forearm on the wooden window-frame and contemplated his reaction to her that afternoon. Surely, it had to be a product of his recent upheavals—the move, travelling, worry over his father and Alexis.

He'd had eight happy years of marriage to Sue-Ellen. He'd loved his wife, damn it. During all the time they'd been together and since she'd died, he hadn't looked at another woman.

Yet one tiny and very public hug with Terri had evoked such a powerful memory that he'd been swept back twelve years to the last time he'd held her in his arms. To a five-minute interlude on the beach.

Ridiculous. Potentially disastrous.

Luke rubbed his jaw, feeling the rasp of stubble. Perhaps he was over-thinking this. Perhaps it merely demonstrated that it was time he did start thinking about a relationship. Or at least start preparing Allie for the possibility that he might one day date. Bring someone, a woman, into the family. He tried to picture that day but long dark silky hair and hot chocolate eyes stayed stubbornly in his mind.

He gave up, let his thoughts dwell on the brief meeting that afternoon. The way Terri had deflected his condolences made him wonder about her. Was her grief still raw? Did she suffer any long-term post-traumatic stress symptoms? A gnawing ache settled in his chest for the pain she'd been through. He could only begin to imagine the difficulty of losing someone the way she had. So brutal and sudden.

He and Allie had had time with Sue-Ellen. Poignant time for words of love, reassurances, promises. Heartbreaking but enriching moments to cling to in the days, weeks, years that followed her death.

Terri hadn't had that. She'd had no chance to say goodbye before her husband had been snatched away.

He needed to be mindful of that, sensitive to her needs, and be ready to offer counselling, in a professional capacity, if she needed it. As hospital director, the welfare of his staff was paramount. He was feeling the natural concern of a doctor for a colleague. Plus Terri wasn't just a colleague, but the sister of a friend. The least he could do was offer support to Ryan O'Connor's sister. Yes, that was more like it. He just needed to apply a bit of sound reasoning.

Through the loosely screening shrubbery, he saw the lights of the cottage come on. Almost as though the intensity of his musings had woken Terri.

He snorted out a small breath. How hopelessly fanciful. So much for the power of common sense.

A few minutes later, she walked across to the hospital in the moonlight. The ends of a stethoscope looped around her neck dangled darkly on her pale T-shirt. She seemed to look up at his window. A queer shaft of excitement made him draw a quick breath before he could block it.

One tiny glance from her and his heart was flopping around in his chest like a freshly caught flounder. He shook his head in disgust.

Terri was obviously the doctor on call tonight.

As his system settled, he watched her disappear through the back door of the hospital and then reappear in the glass-walled corridor. By angling his head, he could follow her progress until she turned the corner leading to Accident and Emergency.

He should go back to bed and yet something held him at the window. A moment later, slow revolutions of light—blue, red, blue, red—began flickering off walls and gutters, signalling the arrival of an emergency vehicle on the other side of the building.

He straightened and, moving quietly, walked back through to the main house to find a T-shirt.

Since sleep was so elusive tonight, he might as well spend the time working with his new colleague. Propinquity in a hospital setting would be the best cure for this inconvenient fascination. Baggy, unflattering clothing, surgical caps, masks, booties. That should take the edge off her appeal quick smart. For his sanity, he needed to start the therapy now. Familiarity bred contempt—he had to believe it.

Anticipation quickened his pace as he retraced her footsteps along the silent hospital corridor.

No sign of any staff in the casualty waiting room. The ambulance was gone. He skirted the main desk and entered the treatment area.

A pale-faced woman sat in an open cubicle clutching a bowl, her eyes closed and head tilted back to rest against the wall.

The nurse attending the woman turned and frowned.

'I'm sorry, sir, you must stay in the waiting room and ring the bell if you need to see the doctor.' She yanked the curtain of the cubicle closed as she came towards him.

'Is Dr Mitchell around?'

'Yes, but you must—'

'I'm Luke Daniels. The new director. And you are?'

'Oh, Dr Daniels.' The line of her mouth thinned even further. 'I'm Dianne Mills, one of the nurses. Terri's busy with an urgent case at the moment.'

'I'm here to help. Where is she?'

'I'll take you through to her.' The woman's subtle unfriendliness seemed to say that his assistance wasn't required or particularly welcome.

Luke smiled grimly as he grabbed a gown from the shelf and followed her. Maybe she was right. Judging by the praise heaped on her by his parents, Terri was a very competent doctor. She'd recognised the signs of his father's myocardial infarct even though Will Daniels had insisted it was just indigestion. What had the stubborn old cuss been thinking? A call to the cardiologist had confirmed that Terri's prompt actions had minimised damage to the cardiac muscle. Tests had shown life-threatening partial occlusions in several other vessels and his father had been whisked in for triple bypass surgery.

'What's the urgent case?' he asked as he tugged the gown over his clothes.

'An unconscious teen brought in by two friends. The girls couldn't wake her when they got her home. We've got food poisoning cases coming in as well. I was just about to call for back-up.' She sent him a speculative look.

'I'll cover.' He smiled. 'We can reassess later with Dr Mitchell if necessary.'

Dianne nodded. Her brief response wasn't encouraging. Perhaps he needed to work on his people skills.

They were still a distance from a closed curtain when Luke heard a young woman's clipped voice say, 'I thought she should sleep it off.'

'But I s-said we should b-bring her here,' added a second, shakier female voice. 'Even th-though it's, like, two o'clock in the morning.'

'You've made the right decision for your cousin.' Terri's even husky tones sent a light shiver over his skin. Sudden doubt needled at the belief that familiarity with her would help him. He swallowed.

'Are you sure she hasn't take anything? Drugs?' Terri asked.

'Um, sh-she—'

'No, of course not,' said the aggressive voice of the first girl. 'Never.'

Luke stepped through the gap in the curtain and took in the situation with a sweeping glance.

Two young women in their late teens stood to one side of a gurney. Dressed to the nines in their party clothes, heavy make-up smudged beneath their eyes and an array of coloured streaks adorned their heads. He caught the tail end of the ferocious glare the taller of the two girls used to browbeat her friend.

Terri's eyes lifted to his briefly in a moment of intense silent communication. It was obvious she didn't believe the girls' denial. Her eyes slid away and she moved to the head of the gurney where she bent over the patient, laryngoscope in hand.

'Temperature up another half-degree to forty-one point five, Terri,' said a nurse as she pulled up the patient's skimpy knitted top and placed the diaphragm of her stethoscope on the pale skin.

'Thanks, Nina.' Terri glanced up. 'Dianne, could you get us some ice packs, stat.'

'On my way.' Dianne slipped out of the curtained cubicle.

Keeping an eye on the activity at the gurney, Luke crossed to the teens. 'I'm Dr Luke Daniels,' he said calmly. 'You're on your way home from a party?'

'A rave.' The taller girl gave him a superior look. She was busily chewing gum and her eyes had the dilated pupils of someone who'd taken some sort of substance. 'Over at Portland.'

'Apical pulse one forty. BP seventy over forty. Sats seventy per cent.' Folding her stethoscope, the nurse turned away to collect a monitor from the side of the room.

Luke turned his attention to the other teen. 'Was your friend able to walk out of the rave on her own?'

'We—we kind of, um, had to h-help her.'

'Was she talking to you then?'

'N-no.'

Out of the corner of his eye, he saw Terri slide in the endotracheal tube.

'Airway in. Ready for the ventilator, Nina.' She straightened, moving aside so the nurse could attach the unit.

Stepping back around the gurney, Terri unwound her stethoscope and listened to both sides of the patient's chest and her abdomen.

Luke looked back at the shorter girl shivering beside him. Deliberately holding her eyes, he said gently, 'We need you to be honest and tell us how long ago she took something. Was it a tablet?'

'Th-three hours.'

'Shona!'

'Well, sh-she did. We all did. They were only l-little pills, j-just to give us a b-boost.'

'Thank you for your honesty,' said Luke, touching her arm to reassure her.

'They were only Es,' said the taller girl, tossing her head. 'There's nothing wrong with me and Shona so it can't be the that.'

'Those so-called party drugs affect everyone differently.' Luke clenched his teeth against the urge to shake some sense into the girl. 'You two have been lucky. You're friend hasn't.'

'J-Jessie had leukaemia. When she was a kid. Is that why she's so sick now?'

A wave of despair at their folly cramped his chest and stomach. He was aware of Terri's eyes on him, but he refused to meet her gaze. He didn't need to see the pity that she undoubtedly felt for him.

'She's g-going to be okay, isn't she?'

'We're doing everything we can for her.' He ushered them towards the curtain. 'We'll get you to wait outside.'

Dianne came back in with cloths and the cold packs.

'I'll organise those, Dianne, thanks,' said Luke, taking them from her. 'Can you show the girls to a room where they can wait, and get next-of-kin information from them, please?'

'C-could we have something to drink?'

Luke met the nurse's concerned eyes. 'A glass of fruit

juice for them, please, Dianne, and perhaps see if there's an apple or two in the staffroom.'

As Dianne showed the girls out, Terri said, 'I'm going to have to set up a central line for fluids.'

'Right. You scrub, we'll monitor Jessie and get your equipment set up,' he said, wrapping the cold packs and placing them in Jessie's groin and armpits.

He'd organised a trolley with the required sterile packs by the time Terri had finished at the sink.

'Gown, gloves.' He nodded to the second trolley.

The soft rustling noises as she gowned up tormented him while he concentrated on opening the catheterisation kit and dropping drapes onto the sterile work surface.

'Do me up, please?'

He turned to see her encased head to toe in surgical green, her elbows bent and gloved hands held relaxed in front of her, maintaining her sterile working space.

He knotted the straps at the nape of her neck, then reached down to do the same at her waist. The warmth he could feel on the tops of his fingers made them clumsy. Try as he may, he couldn't close his mind to the enticing curve of the small of her back.

She turned to face him.

Brown eyes, huge and dark, stared at him from above her mask. His breathing hitched. He was a fool to think hospital clothing would instantly dissolve Terri's appeal. He'd never seen anyone look quite as...*sexy* while preparing for an aseptic procedure.

'Luke?'

He blinked, looked down to see she was handing him the tab for the outside string. She turned in front of him and took back the string. 'Thanks.'

He swallowed. Perhaps he *should* have gone back to

bed after all. Let Dianne call in the emergency back-up. Turning away, he snipped across the shoulder of Jessie's top, exposing her clavicle and neck.

Nina came back with a bag of saline and began to set up the drip monitor.

A moment later, Dianne stuck her head around the curtain. 'I've got contact details for Jessie's mother. They're down from Melbourne, staying with relatives for the weekend.'

'Thanks, Dianne. I'll make the call now.' He took the paper from her and went to the phone. With the line ringing at the other end, Luke tucked the receiver under his ear.

'Terri, the ambos are at your uncle's place,' Dianne said. 'He's aggressive and hypotensive. They're concerned about trying to establish an IV so I suggested they scoop and run.'

'Good idea,' Terri said. 'How's Mary going with the rest of the race-picnic follow-ups?'

'All done now,' Dianne said. 'She's just managed to get through to Matt in Garrangay about the Macintoshes. I'll go and set up a cubicle for your uncle.'

'Thanks, Dianne,' Terri said. 'Nina, can you see if there's any word from the lab tech on call? We'll really need to be able to run some bloods through tonight.'

'Will do.'

Luke pressed redial when the ring tone timed out. With the receiver held to his ear he turned to look in Terri's direction. Her work was quick, neat, methodical. He congratulated himself on being able to view her nimble fingers with detachment. Sure, she was a pleasure to watch but, then, he always enjoyed seeing someone perform a task well. The peculiar feelings that keep threatening to muddle his mind when he was close to her, had to be a product of his stressful few weeks organising his trip back here.

'Hello?' The sleepy voice pulled his attention back to the phone. A short time later, he hung the receiver back on the wall cradle and allowed himself a brief moment to close his eyes. Weariness washed through him as his sympathy went out to Jessie's mother. What a nightmare for a parent.

He straightened and turned around to find Terri's eyes on him as she stripped off her gloves and mask. The beauty she brought to the everyday movements stopped the words in his mouth.

'She's on her way in?'

'Yes.' He cleared his throat, relieved when muscles moved back to normal function. Stepping back to the side of the gurney, he said, 'Her brother's bringing her in.'

Terri moved to stand beside him. Even with the pervasive smells of the hospital, he was piercingly aware of the subtle scent of soap she brought with her. Of her vitality, her fine-boned femininity, the warmth in her dark eyes.

'This must have been a hard case for you on your first night here.'

His mind abruptly went back to the night of the kiss, the parallels with the sympathy she'd shown him then. He wanted it just as little now. He wasn't sure what it was that he did want from her—but he knew it wasn't that.

He rolled his shoulders. 'It's always hard seeing someone as young as Jessie taking risks like this with the rest of her life.'

'Yes.' Her lashes lowered, but not before he'd seen a quick flash of hurt at his brush-off.

An apology hovered on his tongue. Instead, he picked up Jessie's chart and began detailing her treatment. 'We're looking at an ICU transfer for her?'

'I haven't made the call yet. The first priority was

getting her stabilised.' Her voice was all cool business. He must have imagined the moment of vulnerability.

He nodded and recorded another complete set of observations. The girl seemed to be holding her own, with her oxygen saturation and blood pressure markedly improved. Her temperature was steady. 'You've done a good job, Terri.'

The curtain rattled beside them. 'Terri, your uncle's two minutes away.'

'Thanks, Dianne. Be right there.'

'You happy to take Mick's case?' Luke asked, glancing at her as he slotted his pen into the shirt pocket under his gown.

'Yes, of course.'

He nodded. 'I'll call the air ambulance, organise Jessie's transfer.'

'The number's on the wall by the phone.' Terri turned to leave. He couldn't stop his gaze from following her for the few paces it took her to clear the cubicle.

He breathed out a sigh, aware of the odd tension ebbing from his body with her disturbing presence gone. His physiology was more like that of a teenager.

He was a grown man.

A widower, with a daughter.

He dragged a hand down his face. The effect she had on him had to wear off.

Soon. For his sanity, it had to be soon.

Terri hurried through the department, confusion churning through her stomach. Luke had shut her out. Just as he had all those years ago on the beach. Well, what had she expected? They weren't friends. Ryan had been his friend. She was just Ryan's bratty little sister. It was probably all the years of hero worship and then that kiss on the beach that made her feel as though she knew Luke better than she did.

She sighed. Still, he'd be good to work for—which was a relief. She could see that much from this short stint. It had been a pleasure the way he'd fitted in so well, picking up the reins, knowing what she needed and facilitating treatment. He'd deferred to her position as the doctor on call while still commanding respect from everyone in the cubicle. The nurses, the teens, herself.

The teens' rebellion had melted away in the face of his charm, information just flowing out of them under his non-judgemental questioning. The way he'd spoken with Jessie's mother had been wonderful, his velvety voice so full of compassion and caring.

And he'd complimented her handling of the case. In all the years of working with Peter, her husband had never done that.

Luke's praise meant a lot.

More than it should.

Not good! Scratch the surface and there was still a really bad case of hero worship going on underneath.

She was going to have to keep clear of him as much as possible—at work and away from it. Which might be difficult as she lived at the bottom of his parents' garden.

Still, she had no reason to think that he would seek her out. She'd been the one doing the chasing all those years ago—even if she hadn't realised it at the time. Things were different now. She wasn't chasing anyone. She had enough on her plate.

To try to find her courage.

To learn to like the woman she was.

CHAPTER THREE

TERRI met the ambulance at the door, desperately trying to look as professional as possible. Her uncle lay still and pale, his beloved face slightly distorted beneath the oxygen mask. A large white dressing was taped to his forehead. Seeing him like this made her heart twist but she pushed the feeling away. He needed her competence now, not her love.

Frank began his handover as they wheeled the trolley through to the treatment room. She was aware of Dianne and the police sergeant following them.

Between them, they transferred him to the hospital gurney.

Frank stepped back and continued his report. 'There was a smashed bottle of beer on the floor. Looks like he'd slipped in it and hit his head on the corner of the sink. I've dressed the laceration on his forehead. It hadn't bled much,' he said. 'We found him sitting against the kitchen cupboard. After we got the go-ahead to scoop and run, all the fight went out of him. He's been as quiet as a lamb.'

'Okay, thanks, Frank.' Terri leaned over her patient, her hand on his shoulder as she tried to rouse him. 'Uncle Mick? Open your eyes if you can hear me.'

The lashes flicked up and his dry lips stretched into a smile that was more of a grimace. He fumbled with the mask and Terri helped him pull it away, noting the sweetish, ketotic odour of his breath.

'Tee.' He used his nickname for her and for some reason that gave her an instant of misgiving. Should she have stayed with Jessie, handed this case over to Luke as he'd offered? 'What're you doing here, love?'

She shook off the doubt. Responsibility for the emergency department was hers tonight. Luke being here was a bonus, not an opportunity to get him to deal with her family. 'Do you remember what happened, Uncle Mick?'

But his eyes closed again and he mumbled an indistinct response.

'BP is ninety over sixty,' said Dianne.

'Right.' Terri slipped her stethoscope on and listened to the irregular rhythm of his heartbeat. 'Let's get an ECG going, please, Dianne.'

As the nurse snipped off his T-shirt and began attaching the leads, Terri slipped a tourniquet on Mick's arm and bent over his hand. After a moment, she moved on to his wrist and then quickly to his elbow. Beneath her fingertips she could feel the tell-tale springiness of a small vein. Good enough to establish an intravenous line? She hoped so. It would be so much quicker and less complicated than putting in a central line. The sooner Mick started rehydrating, the sooner they could get him stabilised. 'I'm going to put a needle in your arm, Uncle Mick.'

She slipped the cannula into place and released the tourniquet, permitting herself a moment of relief as she taped it securely. She carefully drew off a syringe of blood. 'How's that ECG looking?'

'Typical hypokalaemic changes,' replied a deep voice.

Luke.

Terri took a breath, willing her heart to settle. Surely Jessie hadn't been picked up already.

'Nina's specialling Jessie,' he said as though he'd read her mind. 'She'll call me if she needs me. The transfer chopper is still half an hour away.'

She glanced over to where he examined the ECG strip. He tilted the readout so she could see the flattened T peaks. 'Thanks. It's what I expected. Let's get him started on normal saline IV with thirty millimoles of potassium.'

'I'm on it.' Dianne pivoted away to the bench.

Luke held out his hand for the syringe. 'The lab tech's in. You'll want a priority on the electrolytes and glucose. When they can for the CBC, urea and creatinine?'

'Yes, please. Thanks.'

She'd just opened her mouth to add a request when he said, 'I'll organise a strip reading for the blood glucose so you can set the insulin infusion.'

'Right.' There it was again—that intuitive understanding of her work rhythm. It was fantastic and a little unnerving. With anyone else, she was sure she'd have revelled in the experience. But because it was Luke, there seemed to be a level of intimacy associated with it that she badly needed to deny. But what could she say? *Stop reading my mind—stop doing such a great job?* Terri shrugged mentally and settled for 'Thanks.'

She turned back to her patient and flicked on her pen torch. 'I'm going to shine a light in your eyes, Uncle Mick.'

She lifted each eyelid and watched as the pupils in the deep brown irises expanded and contracted readily. Equal and reactive. At least it looked like he didn't have a head injury to complicate things further.

'Blood sugar, twenty-three,' said Luke.

'Okay.'

Dianne appeared beside her. The nurse reeled off the potassium level in the saline bag then held it so Terri could check the label.

'Correct,' Terri said.

She walked around to the other side of the gurney so she could more easily examine the wound on his forehead. 'I want to have a look at your cut, Uncle Mick.'

'Fluids set, Terri,' said Dianne.

'Thanks.'

A jagged flap of skin had curled back from the triangular laceration but the area looked quite clean. A simple irrigation and suturing job.

'No! No!' Her quiescent patient erupted into unexpected action. So quick. One moment she was lifting the dressing and the next she was flying across the room. In slow motion she watched the horror on Frank and Dianne's faces from the other side of the gurney, their hands uselessly reaching towards her. She saw the sergeant step forward, his mouth tight as he restrained her flailing patient.

Any moment now she was going to hit the floor. Paradoxical that she had so much time to notice everyone's expressions but none to organise her limbs to save herself from the inevitable painful sprawl.

But it didn't happen.

Hands reached her, catching her from behind, cradling her against a hard, warm body. Her uncle lay back down in the milliseconds in which she struggled to understand what had happened. She turned her head and looked up into Luke's grim face. How had he managed to get across the room to save her?

'Are you all right?'

Pain bloomed in her cheekbone, replacing the numbness

of a second ago. His face dissolved and she realised her eyes were tearing up. 'Yes. Thanks.'

She tried to move away but his hands held her firmly, preventing her escape. Short of an undignified struggle, she was helpless to free herself. Luke was so large and hot and solid. She felt fragile. Insubstantial. Utterly feminine.

Though it must have only been seconds, time seemed elastic, stretching to allow her to feel every square inch of contact. He turned her slightly. She could feel his bracing arm behind her back, the fingers that curved around the top of her arm.

'Go and get some ice on that.' He sounded gruff. His eyes, still fixed on her face, were dark.

She blinked the tears into submission, embarrassed at this sign of weakness. 'I have a patient to attend to.'

'I'm taking over.'

'I need to—'

'You need to stand down and let someone else handle this, Dr Mitchell.' His voice lowered, losing its sternness. 'I can feel you trembling, Terri. You need to go and sit down.'

Her defiance ebbed away, making her realise how shaken she felt. 'Yes. Okay.'

He frowned suddenly and tilted his head to look at her more closely. His fingers tightened on her flesh. 'You have a slight nosebleed.'

'Do I?' As soon as she spoke, she could feel the trickle just below her nostril. Knowing there was physical evidence of her injury made her feel even more vulnerable. An uncomfortable sensation.

She pulled out of his grip and this time he released her.

'Go and clean up. I'll finish here then come and have a look at you.' He turned back to her uncle on the gurney.

She hesitated briefly, then realised that the others had

meshed into a team around Luke to treat her uncle. She spun on her heel and left the room.

'I found you at last.'

At the sound of Luke's voice from behind her, Terri jumped. The boxes of twelve-gauge needles she'd been handling scattered across the shelf.

'I wasn't hiding,' she said, not entirely truthfully. How long had he been standing there, watching her?

'Hmm. How are you feeling?'

'I'm fine.' When she'd re-stacked the boxes and re-gained some of her composure, she turned. He was leaning against the doorjamb, his arms folded, one foot crossed over the other. A plain black T-shirt stretched over the chest she'd so recently been clamped against.

'Good. Let's have a look at you, then, shall we?' A slow smile curved his mouth as though he read her reluctance and thought it amusing.

'I don't think *we* need to. But thank you anyway,' she said, shooting him a discouraging stare.

She'd never appreciated how absurdly claustrophobic the long narrow room was with the well-stocked shelves towering along the walls. It was all his fault, of course, the way he was blocking the only exit.

'I think *we* might let *me* be the judge of that.' His smile took on a distinctly determined edge. 'Just think of it as my self interest.'

Terri picked up her clipboard and hugged it tightly in front of her torso. 'Self interest? In what way?'

'If I don't think you're up to it, I'll take over the rest of your shift.'

He waited with an expression of polite interest as she thought of and discarded several weak excuses.

'Oh, all right. Let's get it over with, then,' she muttered. The thought of his hands on her, even in a professional capacity, was nerve-racking. The imprint of their earlier contact still plagued her. Her back to his chest, his fingers on her arms as he turned her…

She forced down a swallow and pushed away the distracting memory. 'Where do you want to do it?'

He raised a brow and his lips tilted.

She felt heat leap through her system. *Oh, God, had she really said that? Please, let the floor open up and swallow her now.* 'The exam.'

'Cubicle three is empty.' Still grinning, he moved to one side and stood with his back pressed against the shelf. Did he think she was going to squeeze past him? No way.

'After you.'

He shrugged. 'Sure.'

She breathed a sigh when he moved but it was short-lived relief. With his back to her, she could appreciate the broadness of his shoulders, the way his torso tapered to his waist and hips, the long, long legs, the easy way he moved. Her mouth felt suddenly dry.

Just outside the door, he turned, looking back at her, one brow raised quizzically. She realised her feet were still planted in the middle of the supply-room floor. Silently cursing her distraction, she tightened her fingers on the clipboard and hurried to catch up.

She walked stiffly to the curtained area, aware of him striding beside her. His lithe, trim body moving smoothly. Unlike her limbs, which felt all angles and awkward gracelessness.

Perched on the edge of the bed, she watched him bend to wash his hands. Her eyes were irresistibly drawn to the denim pulling over the line of his buttocks. When he straightened to rip a piece of paper towel from the dispenser, she looked away quickly.

As he stepped in front of her, she let the deep breath she'd taken trickle out. This was a professional examination, one colleague of another.

Hospital director of staff doctor.

It would only take a few minutes.

'Look past me. You know the drill, hmm? Focus on a point on the wall.' He raised his hand and shone a thin beam of light into her eyes.

'Have you had bleeding from the nose before?'

'Um, a couple of times.' She was acutely aware of his face near hers as he assessed her pupil.

'Recently?'

'No.'

'How long ago?' He moved to her other eye and again bent towards her to do the examination.

'Oh, um. Years.' Then she remembered the exact occasion.

The landmine blast which had killed Peter.

And killed her future. Nausea rushed down on her, sweat popped out of her pores leaving her clammy and chilled. 'It…was…um, a—a couple of years.'

There was a small silence.

'Are you all right, Terri? You've gone very pale.'

The blood abruptly rushed back to her head, filling her face with heat, sweeping away the faintness.

'Yes. Yes. Really, I'm fine.' At least he hadn't commented on her stumbling hesitation. 'You—you asked about nosebleeds. It's been a couple of years.'

'Nothing since?' He frowned as he straightened up, seeming to weigh her response for dissimulation.

She looked away from the measuring blue eyes. The last of the nausea receded. 'No.'

'How heavy were your previous bleeds?'

She frowned and pulled back, pulling herself together at the same time. 'I've had a tiny nosebleed here, not an arterial haemorrhage.'

'Yes, of course.' He appeared to shake himself mentally as he slipped the penlight back into his top pocket. 'I'm going to examine your cheek.'

'Fine,' she said through tight lips, closing her eyes, hoping to shut him out, so close, so threatening to her peace of mind. A rustle of fabric, the tiniest feather of air across her skin. Had he moved closer? Just the thought made her heart kick into a frantic, irregular rhythm. She was too scared to open her eyes to check.

A few tense seconds passed. Why didn't he just get on with it?

Then the subtle torture began. Gentle probing fingers travelled down her nose, across her cheekbone, around her eye socket.

Nasal bone, glabella, maxilla, zygomatic.

Breathe in and out. In and out. Perhaps if she recited the muscles. There were so many of them…

She couldn't think of a single name.

Closing her eyes had been a bad idea. Sure, it meant she couldn't see him but the other sensory information was overwhelming. The heat of his body reached out to her. His smell—part soap, part tantalising masculine musk—surrounded her. Small whispery sounds of each inhalation, exhalation. How much more measured and normal his breathing was than hers.

His touch was warm and deft. The skin beneath his fingertips was alive with nerve endings. Nearby cells seemed to quiver in anticipation of their turn.

She swallowed, feeling so thoroughly shaken now that she didn't dare open her eyes lest he read her ragged state.

Think of something else. Now!

Work. The emergency department.

'How's Uncle Mick?' she said, dismayed to hear her breathlessness.

'Uncle Mick?' He sounded preoccupied. 'Oh, yes. Mick.'

After a moment, he cleared his throat. 'I'm just waiting for the blood results to come back. Particularly the sodium level. I noticed you had a half-strength saline bag standing by.'

'Yes.' She pushed the answer out, working hard to keep her tone even. Concentrate on work, on the technicalities. That would surely bring her back to an even keel. 'I was worried about hyperosmolar hyperglycaemia.'

His fingers stopped moving, the tips resting softly on her skin. The moment hung, oddly alive with possibilities. Had he finished?

Finally, she opened her eyes and looked straight into his, so close. He looked almost puzzled. His pupils were huge, making his eyes dark and intense. For a second, she thought she read a match to her own helpless awareness in the inky depths. Was it real? Or was she desperately trying to see something so she'd feel better? Something to tell her that she wasn't the only one caught by this sensual spell?

Hard on the heels of that thought, she realised it would be better if the weakness was hers alone. How much more difficult might it be to resist the temptation to explore this if she knew he felt the same way.

'Dr Daniels?' Dianne's voice broke the spell.

Shock shuddered all the way to Terri's toes.

Luke snatched his hands away from her face as though she were contaminated. He blinked and the earlier, intense look was gone. Now his expression was easy to read. Shock, plain and simple.

'The lab's just rung through the results for the sodium and blood sugar on Mick Butler,' said Dianne, seeming not to notice anything amiss.

Terri felt heat rushing to her face. She wanted nothing more than to cover her cheeks with her hands. Bowing her head, she brushed a crease on her scrubs.

'Results. Yes. Good.' Luke cleared his throat. His apparent discomfort was a small balm to Terri's frazzled system. 'Er, what are they?'

'Sodium, one hundred and forty. Glucose, twenty-four.'

'Right. Thanks, Dianne.' The rasp had gone from his voice. 'We won't need to change to the half-strength normal saline.'

Out of the corner of her eye, Terri saw him dig his hands into his jeans pockets.

'How's your nose, Terri?' asked Dianne. 'That was a real thump Mick gave you.'

'I'm fine.' Terri looked up, making her lips stretch into what she hoped was a reassuring smile. 'No lasting damage. Just a bit tender.'

'Are you sure?' Dianne's hazel eyes searched her face.

'Yes.' Oh, God, think of something to say, before Dianne says anything else. The woman was a fantastic emergency department nurse but no diplomat. But Terri's rattled brain didn't produce anything in time.

'You're looking very flushed. Almost feverish. Do you think you've got a temperature? Will you be all right to stay on duty?'

Terri scowled as she slipped off the bed. 'Yes, of course I'll be right to work the rest of the shift. If I look flushed it's because the two of you are looking at me as though

I'm something squashed on a microscope slide. Perhaps you could both take yourselves off and find some other poor specimen to peer at.'

Unconcerned by the tart response, Dianne grinned then delivered her parting comment. 'You're going to have a shiner.'

'Such a good look for an accident and emergency doctor,' Terri muttered. She glanced at Luke. 'Are you going home now?'

'Will you be okay for the rest of the night?' His voice was low and warm.

'Yes, of course,' she said briskly. She needed to take herself in hand. His concern was *professional*. She couldn't let that lovely, rich voice fill her with this inappropriate neediness. 'Thanks for your help and, um, for catching me.'

'No problems.' He smiled briefly. 'I'll leave you to it, then.'

She watched him go. If her roiling confusion was anything to judge by, it was going to be a physically and mentally draining twelve months.

Perhaps it was time to consider moving on. Her contract only had six months left. But she didn't *want* to move. She'd been thinking about extending her contract. It felt wonderful to be home. Comfortable, safe, reassuring after the trauma she'd been through. It felt like the best place for her while she got back on her feet.

Port Cavill had everything. Wonderful people, gorgeous setting, a great hospital, a world-class motorcycle track.

Unfortunately, it also had Luke.

But it only had Luke for a year. Could she survive that long?

CHAPTER FOUR

TERRI'S cottage door was open but there was no answer to his knock. Through the window, Luke could see the small sitting room. A subdued golden glow from the lamp made it cosy and welcoming in the dusk. A far cry from the cramped and messy look he'd cultivated while using the cottage as his bachelor pad in his late teens.

He hesitated. She couldn't be far away, perhaps down on the beach. Should he follow her down there? Perhaps he should take her absence as an opportunity to slide away unnoticed. He'd been calling himself all the fools under the sun for coming down here anyway...

But when his feet moved it was to follow the path around the cottage, past her bike tucked in the rickety garage.

The shushing of waves grew steadily louder as he approached the line of trees edging the grounds. He picked his way through the grove and paused on the open sand, breathing in the salty tang of the ocean. Moonlight washed the scene with a ghostly aura.

A short distance away, Terri stood at the edge of the water, her hands tucked into the back pockets of her jeans. A floppy knitted top clung to her slender curves. Her head tilted slightly as she stared out to sea. She paid no heed to the wave ripple creeping towards her naked toes. At the last moment it paused and slid away again without daring to touch.

She seemed lonely, sad. He had a powerful urge to reach out to her, to offer comfort. Or was it something else?

He'd kissed her on this very spot. Hard to believe it was a dozen years in the past. He could remember how she tasted. Sweet with a promise of spice.

'Remember the night of the schoolies' party?' The question was out before he could think better of it. She had a powerful effect on him—a walk down memory lane with her was a torment he could do without. Besides, that night didn't reflect well on him.

'Of course.' Slowly, she turned her head to look at him. Dark shadows from the bruising beneath her eyes made her look mysterious, almost exotic, reminding him how little he knew about her.

'I wasn't kind to you that night.' He'd wanted to take what she'd offered…and more. Much more. He'd wanted to grab, to hold on, to lose himself in her sweetness, her gentle sympathy. Somehow, he'd found the sanity and strength to pull back, to send her away.

But he hadn't done it graciously.

She shrugged and looked away. 'I wasn't asking for your kindness. I only wanted to talk to you about getting a medical degree.'

'I know.' He frowned. Had the kiss that came back to haunt him after all these years meant nothing to her? She sounded so indifferent that he felt an inexplicable urge to push, to get a reaction from her. 'I'm surprised I didn't put you off.'

'You weren't that bad.' She took her hands out of her pockets and bent to pick something up.

He swallowed, unable to look away from the unconscious provocation of jeans pulled tight against her curved buttocks. The knitted top rode up, exposing a small wedge of pale skin, gone in a flash as she straightened. She bent to examine a curved shell in her long fingers, her face hidden by a curtain of wavy dark hair. It was a little shorter now than it had been when he'd buried his fingers in it twelve years ago.

He pulled his mind back to the conversation.

'Wasn't I?' Perhaps the incident loomed much larger in his mind because sobriety the following day had brought sneaking shame at his behaviour. 'That isn't how I remember it.'

'You were grieving for your cousin.' She slanted him a look as she pushed the thick curls back over her shoulder.

'This must be a first for gender interaction.' He huffed out a small laugh, feeling irrationally frustrated with her. 'I'm trying in a roundabout way to apologise for the things I said and you're busy making excuses for me. I took my anger out on you.'

She grinned at him, her teeth gleaming in the subdued light. 'Would you feel better if I said you'd been callous and cruel and I've never recovered? That I'm bitter and twisted with an abiding fear of beaches?'

He felt suddenly foolish. 'Maybe not.' But he realised that some tiny part of him wanted a sign that their exchange on that long-ago evening had meant something to her…even as he recognised his folly.

Her hands tipped the shell from palm to palm as she contemplated him for a moment. 'Want to walk?' she said, waving a hand vaguely along the beach. 'Just along to the rocks and back.'

'Sure.' He levered off his runners and hooked his fingers into the heels. Sand sifted between his toes in a soft caress. When Terri moved away, he fell into step with her.

The gentle sibilance of the waves filled a small silence. He felt an odd mixture of relaxation and intense awareness of every move that she made.

'You said something important to me that night.' Her voice was deliciously husky, easy to listen to.

'Now I *am* worried. Wisdom brewed in a beer bottle.' He grimaced. Should he be embarrassed or pleased that she apparently remembered something after all? 'What pearl did I drop?'

'That one of the hardest lessons is not being able to save everyone.'

'Ah. Yes.' An echo of his harsh feelings trickled through his memory. Such bitterness and anger at the senselessness of his cousin's death. What chance had Terri had to soothe his pain? Yet she'd tried after he'd pushed everyone else away. And she'd succeeded to a degree. Their kiss had distracted him. It was that he remembered most clearly about that night, not his grief.

'You were right. Failure can be hard to live with.' She sounded sombre. Was she thinking about her husband? Had she tried to save him after the explosion? He was trying to frame a diplomatic question when she said, 'You were talking about Kevin, weren't you?'

A shadow darkened his mood for a moment. His cousin had been young, full of promise, full of male bravado—a reflection of himself. 'Mmm. I was still pretty raw.'

She tilted her head to look at him. 'You were very close?'

'We grew up together.' The simple sentence couldn't begin to describe their relationship. His throat grew thick.

'Mum used to say that we were more like twins than cousins.'

They reached the rocks and silently turned to retrace their steps.

She stopped to throw the shell into the water then scrubbed her hands together. When she turned her gaze met his. 'Dad said you were working on Kevin when he arrived at the scene.'

He'd forgotten that her father had been the local police sergeant at the time. It'd been her father who had pulled him away from Kevin's body when the paramedics had arrived. A band of stiffness tightened around his larynx. He cleared his throat. 'It wasn't enough.'

In the small pause that followed, he watched a wave ebb, its highest point marked by a thin line of froth. 'I felt responsible for the accident.'

'Why?' Her voice held only curiosity. Nothing more. Would she judge him when she knew the whole story? Every now and then he still wondered if he'd done things differently, if he'd picked his words more carefully…but thinking that way was pointless.

He flexed his shoulders, feeling the old weight of his dereliction. 'We'd argued about his recklessness. Kevin rode as though he was immortal.' He lifted his eyes back to hers. 'Hell, I suppose we both did. He didn't even make it through the first bend. I saw him hit the car head on.'

'Oh, Luke.' He could hear her distress, felt unexpectedly soothed by the knowledge it was for him.

'I grew up after that.'

'It wasn't your fault.' She put her hand on his arm.

He stared down into her eyes for a long second, feeling his heart twist. 'Still got that soft heart, haven't you, Terri? I know it wasn't my fault…now. At the time…' He shrugged.

After a moment, he reached out to stroke her cheek, her skin soft and cool beneath his fingertips. She shivered and desire punched into him, shortening his breath, tightening his gut.

Would she resist if he pulled her close? Folded her into his body? Covered her lips with his?

Finished what they'd started all those years ago. Right here. Right now.

The connection stretched. Then she snatched her hand back, removing it from his elbow, and folded her arms.

He dragged in a huge breath and took a mental step back. 'You're cold. We should go in.'

'Yes.' Head down, she made a beeline for the trees at the top of the beach. Almost as though she was trying to escape. Had she sensed the desperation with which he'd held himself in check?

He smiled grimly. Surely if she had, she'd be running.

The silence between them wasn't comfortable. Touching her had created a tension that hadn't dissipated even though the physical link had broken.

'So how are you settling in? And Alexis?' Terri sounded slightly out of breath. Still because of him? Or was it the cracking pace she'd set?

He grasped at her change of subject, relieved one of them was functioning above waist level.

'Okay.' He thought of yesterday's asthma attack and the dramatics which had preceded it. 'Allie says I've blighted her young life by dragging her halfway around the world to the back of beyond. She wanted me to leave her behind with one of her friends.'

'She must miss them,' Terri said softly.

'We're only here for a year. She'll make new friends if she gives herself the chance.' He was dismayed by the defensiveness he could hear in his voice in reaction to Terri's gentle compassion for his daughter. Frustration mixed with self-disgust. At least talking about this took his mind off the other source of frustration walking up the sandy path ahead of him. *Though not entirely*. Even in the dim light, he could see Terri's slender hips swaying in her pale jeans.

'What are her hobbies?'

'Hobbies? Oh, hobbies. Yes.' *God, get a grip, man.* What were his daughter's hobbies? 'Soccer. She plays soccer.'

'There's a junior soccer league she can join.'

He reached up to push a low branch out of the way. 'Actually, that's a damned good idea. Thanks.'

'A year's a long time when you're her age,' she said a few steps later.

'It'll be a bloody long time when you're *my* age if she's going to sulk for the whole time.'

Terri chuckled.

'Thanks for the sympathy,' he muttered, holding back a self-deprecating smile.

'Sorry. I'm not really laughing at you.' Kind humour mixed with the understanding in her soft words. 'It must be difficult for both of you.'

'Mmm. I'm only being spoken to when she can't avoid it. The way she's behaving I'll need to get her intensive counselling to recover. Maybe I should book some for myself while I'm at it.' He was making light of the situation but his heart was weighed down by the knowledge of his daughter's unhappiness. There was no way around it. He was committed to helping his father for this year.

'I'm sure you'll work it out.' Terri stepped onto the veranda of the cottage. 'Well, this is my stop.'

He should go but her obvious relief made him push his welcome. Just for a few minutes more. A chance to work on his familiarity plan, give it another opportunity to kick in. Besides, he needed the small respite before facing the tension back at the house. 'I wouldn't say no to a cup of coffee.'

Her pleased look faded. He suppressed a smile and waited.

'Wouldn't you?' She turned her head slightly as though she made a quick inventory of the rooms. It made him wonder what she didn't want him to see, but all she said was, 'You'd better come in, then.'

'Thanks.'

They wiped the sand off their feet at the door.

'It'll just be instant,' she said, glancing at him as he followed her into the compact kitchen.

In the artificial light, he clearly saw the purple-blue smudges forming under both her eyes and a faint bruise on the bridge of her nose.

'Coffee.' She froze with the jar clutched to her chest as he stepped closer. 'What are you doing?'

'How's your nose?' Cupping her face, he tilted it to the light. Her carotid pulse jumped against the edge of his hands. Masculine satisfaction surged through him.

'Fine.'

'No sign of any problems after last night?' Her skin felt soft and smooth beneath his finger tips.

'No. None.' She scowled. 'Have you finished?'

Was he? His gaze dropped to her mouth. If he leaned forward, just a little, he would discover if reality was as delicious as his memories of their kiss. Temptation wrestled with good sense.

Then the opportunity was gone as Terri pulled back out of his light hold.

'You won't get your coffee unless you get out of my kitchen,' she said tartly. 'Why don't you sit at the table?'

He stifled a sigh and retreated, slipping onto one of the chairs and allowing himself to follow her with his eyes. Watching her was like indulging in a visual feast. Filling the jug, getting out the mugs, spooning in the coffee. Commonplace, everyday things.

But there was nothing commonplace about his reaction. He shifted on the chair, easing the snugness of his jeans. To take his mind off her, he looked around the room. Ochre walls made the little room cheerful. At the end of the bench a distressed dresser displayed an eclectic collection of china. The cupboards had been stripped back and varnished to show off the warm grain of Baltic pine.

'You've made the place nice. A vast improvement on when I lived here.'

'Thanks.' She smiled slightly and switched off the jug. 'I must admit I prefer butterscotch paint to wall-to-wall centrefolds.'

'God, were they still up?' An unexpected wave of self-consciousness threatened to heat his face as though he was an awkward adolescent.

'Every single anatomically enhanced one of them.' She slid him a cheeky look. 'If I'd known you were coming back I could have saved them for you.'

He snorted, his momentary embarrassment evaporating. 'I like my women more natural these days.' *Like you.* The unspoken words reverberated in his head.

She smirked at him, obviously comfortable again now that he was at a distance. The devil in him wanted to see that composure shaken again, to know that he wasn't the only one affected by this inconvenient attraction. 'There's another reason why I was so hard on you that night on the beach.'

She eyed him warily. 'There was?'

'Oh, yeah,' he drawled. 'I fancied the pants off you.'

'No!' Her mouth opened in a perfect circle of shock. She blinked at him then burst out laughing. Nervous laughter that only lasted for a moment before she stopped and stared at him again.

'Yes.' He grinned, enjoying her reaction.

'Oh, come on.' Her movements were jerky as she turned back to the bench to pick up a spoon. The staccato clatter of metal on china filled the room. He could imagine her marshalling her defences. After a moment, she said, 'You barely knew who I was.'

'Oh, I knew all right,' he murmured as she turned with the hot drinks in her hand. The only sign remaining of her agitation was the heightened colour in her cheeks. 'You used to haunt your uncle's racetrack.'

She handed him a steaming mug.

'Thanks.' He considered her over the rim as he took a small sip. 'Your brother warned me off.'

'Ryan? Did he?' She wrinkled her nose in disbelief.

'Sure. He warned off a few of us. He'd have dismembered me if he'd known some of the things I'd thought about you.' Things he'd have liked to share with her... would still like to share with her.

'I never realised. I must make sure I thank him for his interference.' She shook her head, her lips curved with amusement. 'And here I thought I was the most unpopular girl in school. All the boys wanted to be my friend but never my *boy*friend.'

'It was self-preservation.' He grinned, raising the mug to take another mouthful. Flirting with her was fun—regardless of whether it was a good idea. It had been a long time since he'd done something just for the fun of it. 'I half expected a visit from your brother after I kissed you that night.'

'You thought I'd run home and tell?' She gave him an old-fashioned look and signalled for him to follow her along the hall. Over her shoulder, she said, 'Why would I advertise the fact that you'd rejected me?'

'I wasn't rejecting you,' he said as she led the way into the lounge.

'Oh, yes? I was kissed by the local heart-throb and then told he didn't want to babysit. That was a rejection in my book.' She curled into one of the overstuffed chairs and looked at him with a small enigmatic smile on her lips.

'Local heart-throb?' His cheeks warmed. This woman could really throw his system for a loop. 'Give me a break.'

'Tsk. *I'm* telling this story, not you.' She waved an airy hand, dismissing his protest. 'My poor seventeen-year-old ego was thoroughly battered.'

Luke grinned at her. 'You seem to have recovered just fine.'

'Some scars don't show.' She arched an expressive brow at him.

He felt his smile slip. God, she was so tempting. The offer to make amends was ready to leap off his tongue. With an effort he stifled the unruly impulse. That was *not* the sort of familiarity he needed to cultivate with Terri.

Shaking himself mentally, he looked around the room, his eyes settling on a collection of photographs on the mantelpiece. He stood and crossed the room to pick up one of the pictures. An unsmiling man stared out of the frame. Tanned, good-looking. Intense. He glanced at Terri. 'Is this your husband?'

'Yes.' Her fingers curled around her mug and she blew on the liquid as though cooling it was the most important thing in the world.

The easy relaxed atmosphere was gone in an instant and he was sorry to have been the one to destroy it. He hesitated then said, 'Mum told me he was killed in a landmine explosion.'

'Yes.' Her monosyllabic answers discouraged further questions. She was obviously troubled and he wanted to get past the barrier she was putting up.

'Yesterday…' He put the picture back and moved to the sofa. 'You cut me off when I was going to offer my condolences.'

She shrugged. 'Nothing will undo what's happened.'

'You were with him when it happened,' he said gently as he sat down.

'Yes.' Her expression was shuttered.

'Were you injured?'

'I walked away.' She hadn't really answered the question and he sensed there was much more to the story.

'It must have been traumatic.'

'You could say that.' She hunched over her mug, resolutely keeping her gaze averted.

The healer in him wanted to help, find the key so she would let him in. Anguish radiated from her and he couldn't let it rest. 'Any ongoing problems?'

Her head snapped up and she glared at him. 'Why? Are you worried about working with me?'

Remembering his own grief after Kevin's death and then with Sue-Ellen, his heart ached for her. 'Maybe I'm worried *about* you, Terri.'

'It's not necessary and it's not your place.' Her lips barely moved as she grated the words out. 'I've done the counselling. Learned to live with it. I don't like giving people, *acquaintances*, chapter and verse on my life's tragedies.'

He ignored the sarcasm, hearing the residue of pain behind it. He knew well the twin burden of grief and guilt. Regrets over Sue-Ellen's death still tugged on his conscience.

'What about friends?' he asked softly. 'We're friends, at least, aren't we?'

She stared at him coolly. A tiny tremble of her chin betrayed her before she set her jaw.

'Well, if you need to talk…' He opened his hands, making a small conciliatory gesture.

'You'll be the first to know,' she said flippantly with a toss of her head.

'I'm sure I won't, but the offer stands. Any time.' He smiled gently. He'd failed to reach her. Worse than that, he suspected he'd caused her more suffering with his well-meant probing.

There was a small silence and then she said, 'Was there a particular reason for your visit tonight, Luke?'

He stifled a sigh. His communication skills with the opposite sex were not good at the moment. He'd alienated Allie and now he was doing the same with a colleague and friend. 'I wanted to see how you were after last night. Plus, we're going to be working together and—'

'So you'll be making these cosy calls on the other staff members as well, will you?' She looked at him then, one eyebrow raised, challenging.

'And I wanted to thank you for taking such good care of Dad with his MI,' he continued smoothly, ignoring her interruption. 'You saved his life.'

Her shoulders moved in a tiny shrug. 'I was just doing my job.'

'I know, but in this case the job was my father so thank you. He was lucky you were at the barbecue when it happened. Mum told me how stubborn he was about his *indigestion.*'

'It's hard for some people to face physical vulnerability. Especially someone as vital as your dad.' She studied the liquid in her mug.

Was she speaking from experience? He couldn't ask, not tonight. He'd already asked too much, definitely worn out his welcome. His heart squeezed and he felt the same frustrating helplessness as when Allie shut him out. The same…but different. This feeling was mixed with a potent attraction. More than anything, he wanted to scoop her into his arms, to comfort and reassure.

Bad idea. They had to work together. For a year. The sexual chemistry between them made it impossible for him to judge where altruism ended and lust began.

He had to keep reminding himself she was a colleague. Keep striving for that day when he'd know her so well this fizz of awareness would be a thing of the past.

The silence was broken by the catarrhal cough of a possum outside.

'I'd better go. Thanks for the coffee.' He placed his mug on the low table and waited a beat. 'I'll let myself out, shall I?'

At the door, he looked back at her. She hadn't moved.

'Goodnight, Terri.' That air of fragility about her tonight was probably entirely in his over-protective imagination.

''Night.'

Terri sat for a long time after Luke left, waiting for her equilibrium to return. Inviting him into this room had been a disaster. Why hadn't she thought of the photographs, realised he might be curious? But at the time she'd only thought of sitting somewhere other than the tiny kitchen table, where their knees would have touched every time they moved. Her eyes touched on the picture of Peter, her hand automatically sliding to her belly.

Protecting where there was nothing left to protect. Tears stung her eyes, pushing to escape. She thought she'd finished with crying…

She'd been wrong.

CHAPTER FIVE

TERRI stared at the now-silent CB receiver in her hand, noting the tremor in her fingers with an odd detachment. The radio unit clattered slightly as she returned it to the base cradle.

A baby. Eight months. Fever of one hundred and two degrees for several hours. Part of her knew she should have suggested continuing with fluids and waiting another couple of hours before coming in. But the rest of her couldn't bear to take the risk.

Not today.

Babies were special, the small lives so precious.

Of their own volition, the fingers of one hand splayed across her abdomen. Her own baby would have been eighteen months old if she hadn't miscarried.

Eyes closed, she bowed her head. Abruptly, her sensory memory delivered a staggering tableau. The pungent stench of cordite clogging her nostrils, Peter's cries ringing in her ears. The cramping pain in her stomach as she'd crawled to try to help him. So much damage, so much blood. The very air had coated the back of her tongue thickly with the metallic taste.

She could still feel the puff of Peter's breath on her ear

as he struggled to talk, to apologise, to ask her to look after their child. In his final moments, a connection between them, one that had all but vanished after they'd married.

A spasm low in her abdomen reminded her how she'd failed them all: Peter, her baby, *herself*.

In the aftermath of the trauma, her body had rejected its precious cargo.

Today was the second anniversary.

'Terri?'

'Luke!' Her eyes flew open and she spun round to face him. 'Luke.'

The room seemed to rock for a second and she put a hand on the bench to steady herself.

He stepped forward, his hand wrapping around her arm above the elbow. The warmth of his fingers a tiny comfort against the chill she felt. Concern filled the blue eyes drilling into hers. 'Are you all right?'

'Oh, yes,' she managed, faintly. Even to her own ears she sounded less than convincing. But she *was* all right...or she would be. He'd just caught her at a vulnerable moment.

'Come and sit down before... Sit down and tell me what the problem is.' His compassionate bedside manner flowed over her, making her want to believe he cared.

She swallowed and stood firm. 'Really, I'm fine.'

In a way, her turmoil was his fault. Talking to him the other night had left her more vulnerable than usual, that was all. His kindness, his offer to help had left her raw. She'd coped so well with the first anniversary. This second one was ambushing her, ruthlessly exposing the cracks in her defences. The skills she had used to keep herself functioning for the past two years felt fragile and unreliable. Twenty-four months. Would any amount of time be long enough to blunt the pain?

Perhaps she'd have taken today in her stride if Luke's visit hadn't unlocked her vault of painful memories, pitching her back into the emotional maelstrom of the tragedy.

But she would get past it, she had to.

'Terri?'

Luke's voice snapped her back to the present and she barely suppressed a start. If she didn't pull herself together, he'd be afraid to have her working in the department tonight. And she needed to work—she couldn't go home and sit alone with her thoughts. She had one constant, her ability to focus on her work. She was good at her job and that wasn't going to stop now. She couldn't let it—work was all she had left.

She took a deep steadying breath. With her eyes on the notes she'd made, she concentrated on the details.

'We've got two patients on the way in. A thirty-year-old male involved in a quad bike accident. Required resuscitation at the scene. He has head, chest and leg injuries.' Her voice was level and calm. No sign of the turmoil so close to the surface.

'Right. And the other patient?'

Her fingers tightened and the paper she held crackled a protest. She swallowed.

'The other patient is a febrile eight-month-old. Some vomiting and diarrhoea with a temperature of a hundred and two for several hours. There's no indication that his case is anything more serious than a childhood fever but I've suggested bringing him in for examination. Mum's extra-anxious because her niece had meningicoccal disease last year. The family live out of town and Dad's away on business so...' She clamped her lips to stop the flow of words. Her reasoning was feeble, the product of personal anxiety rather than professional concern. She needed to marshal a better argument.

'So you didn't want to leave Mum isolated in case things deteriorate during the night?' Luke shrugged. 'That's part of the reason we're here, isn't it? Better to have a patient come in and prove to be a minor case than to have us miss something major.'

Terri opened her mouth to defend her case for having the child brought in and then his words sank in. He wasn't questioning her decision, as she'd expected…as she deserved.

'Um, yes.' Grateful as she was for his attitude, the quick acceptance of her position made her feel like an inexperienced rookie. She suppressed a sigh and acknowledged the truth—the mood she was in tonight meant that whatever response Luke made, she would be hard to please.

She set the paper aside and glanced at her watch. 'The ETA on the quad bike victim is any minute now. The febrile infant will be at least twenty minutes.'

As soon as she'd finished speaking an ambulance glided up to the entrance, red and blue lights revolving.

'Let's get to work,' he said grimly, heading for the door.

With Luke's attention directed towards the unconscious patient being unloaded by the paramedics, Terri felt a subtle release of tension in her muscles. The quiet air of strength and competence that he radiated should have made him a pleasure to work with…it *did* make him a pleasure to work with, but it was also subtly threatening.

He saw too much and she had secret agonies she couldn't bear to have exposed. He'd already encroached where no one else had by asking her about the explosion that had killed Peter. Other people tiptoed around the issue, relieved when she moved the conversation away to safer topics. But not Luke. Had he sensed there was a problem?

She had to find the resolve to keep him out, not let his compassion weaken her. The guilt and responsibility, the burden for the terrible loss was hers and hers alone.

Luke watched the diminishing lights of the helicopter ambulance for a moment longer before turning wearily to walk back into the hospital. The future of the quad-bike victim was in the neurosurgeon's hands now.

The man's wife had wanted absolute reassurances that he'd recover but Luke couldn't give them to her. Even if her husband survived, he'd probably have months of rehabilitation ahead of him.

He and Terri had done everything they could. The skull X-ray had shown an intracranial haematoma, as he'd suspected from the blown right pupil. With the help of a telephone consult to a Melbourne neurosurgeon, they'd evacuated an epidural clot through a burr-hole. They weren't ideally set up for the procedure but they'd had to do it as soon as possible for the man to have any chance of a full recovery. Now stabilised, with the pressure on his brain released, the accident victim was on his way to facilities where he could be monitored by regular CT scans.

The only good thing about the situation was that the couple's five-year-old daughter had hopped off the bike moments before the performance of the tragic stunt.

Luke stripped off his blood-stained gown, lobbing it into the laundry bin beside the sink before scrubbing his hands.

He wondered how Terri was getting on with the dehydrated infant.

Odd how she'd behaved earlier when he'd first come on shift. She'd been so obviously upset that all his protective instincts had gone on high alert, demanding that he do something, anything, to help. After avoiding him for the best part of a week, she'd seemed positively delighted to see him. A disproportionate leap of pleasure had rushed through him in that split second when she'd turned to look at him, her eyes shining. Until she'd put her hand out on the bench to steady herself and he'd seen the desperation underlying her veneer of composure. For a moment, he'd been afraid she was going to collapse at his feet.

But there'd been no sign of hesitation or diffidence when she'd helped him with the quad-bike trauma case. He'd watched for it, been ready to take over if she'd faltered. But she'd been great. Better than great.

She'd been fantastic since day one, taking direction from him with no hostility at all. After his father had explained to him the hospital board's poor handling of the filling of the position he'd wondered how their working relationship would function. But it was a pleasure...in every way. And if there were any undertones of resentment, he couldn't detect them. If anything, he was the one giving out the mixed signals.

He enjoyed working with her. And on a personal level, he enjoyed being close to her. Perhaps just a little too much. Since that first night when he'd had his hands on her, he'd wanted nothing more than to touch her again.

Professionally, it was a potential time bomb.

She impressed the hell out of him.

As a doctor, she was strong and competent.

As a woman, she was an enigma. One he wanted to solve. The more he *knew* about her the less he understood her.

Those occasional flashes of uncertainty and fragility he saw in her cut straight to his heart. They were so out of keeping with the rest of her.

What had upset her tonight? Obviously not the trauma patient. Could it have been the infant?

It didn't make sense. That case appeared to be so straight-forward. Perhaps Terri had been a little on the cautious side but he preferred that in the staff he worked with than someone who was negligent about cases.

He knew Terri had taken the infant and her mother through to one of the double rooms. The woman had a toddler to look after as well and Terri's suggestion of a family room for them had made sense. His runners made no noise as he padded through to the quiet corridor

At the door of the room, he stopped dead.

Terri held the happy chortling baby on her knee. He could see her profile, see the loving smile on her lips. The boy's trusting eyes looked up into Terri's face as a stream of unintelligible words tumbled out of the rosebud mouth. The fingers of one chubby hand wrapped around Terri's thumb and he tried to stuff it between his lips.

'Aren't you a gorgeous wee man?' cooed Terri, her voice a warm, maternal caress. Luke's breath choked up in his throat.

'Ga!' said the child, responding enthusiastically to her tone.

'Yes, you are.'

The sight rocked Luke to the core, raising age-old masculine instincts to protect, to possess. He swallowed hard, waiting for the world to settle.

He adored being a father. From the moment he'd laid eyes on his daughter, his soul had been filled by her sweet invasion of his life.

A sharp, uncomfortable hunger stirred in his heart as he watched Terri with the child.

He must have made a small noise because Terri looked

up suddenly. Her smile was filled with a warm uncompli-cated love that slammed into him. The charged moment was packed with intimacy. His heart made a slow painful revolution in his chest and a shudder of recognition fizzed through his brain.

He wanted…He refused to let his mind finish the thought.

Terri's smile faltered and he wondered what she read on his face. Then she blinked, and a quick puzzled look filled her lovely dark eyes before she looked away. She was still seated in front of him but he had the oddest feeling she'd withdrawn from him, mentally fled.

He moved closer, compelled by a wholly male desire to pursue.

'Someone's looking a lot happier.' He sat beside her, putting one hand on the back of her chair as he leaned towards the child. He suppressed a grin when Terri flicked him a wary look. Her senses were spot on. Though he tried to present an unthreatening appearance, she had stirred a primitive corner within him.

He smiled as he stroked the baby's soft cheek with the back of one finger. The small mouth drooled saliva as it made chewing motions on Terri's knuckle. 'Teething as well, is he?'

'Yes. Which is possibly why he wasn't settling for his mum.' Her voice was soft and tender. 'Poor little fellow.'

Luke's eyes were drawn to Terri's profile. She wore her hair up twisted in a loose bun on the crown of her head, making it easy for him to study her profile, the curve of her cheek, the neat straight nose, stubborn chin.

Another wave of need spiralled through his gut. He hadn't felt such compelling sexual awareness for a long time. Experiencing it now so powerfully was exciting and unnerving.

He had some thinking to do. His situation with Terri was a sensitive one. He was her boss, they worked in a small hospital. They were both here for a limited time.

But there was something between them. Would Terri allow him to pursue it?

Or perhaps the more important question was, was pursuing it wise?

'Come on, kiddo. You can't sit there all day.'

Luke's head lifted at the sound of his sister's voice coming from just outside his line of sight. He knew Allie was reading a book on the patio. His fingers paused on the pawn he'd been about to move as he strained to hear his daughter's mumbled response. He picked up his father's black knight and left his piece on the square.

Not deterred, Megan chirped, 'It's time for some girl stuff. Let's go and see if Terri's home.'

Terri. A hot thrill streaked through him before he could suppress it. Sharp angles on the chess-piece dug into his palm as his fingers clenched around it. God, he had it bad if just her name being spoken unexpectedly could affect him like this.

'I don't know if Dad will let me.' Allie sounded bored and sulky.

'You won't know unless you ask him, will you, bunny? Come on. He's just inside playing chess with Dad.' Megan stuck her head around the corner of the French door. 'Hey, Luke, I'm going down to see Terri. Okay if Allie comes with me?'

His daughter's head appeared beside Megan's, her face anxious. Was she worried about going? Or worried he wouldn't let her? Everyday life required the skills of a wiser man than he.

'Do you want to, Allie?' he asked, keeping his tone neutral.

'I guess, sure. It's not like there's anything else to do.' She shrugged, trying to look nonchalant, but he'd seen the gleam of interest in her eyes. More than he'd seen in a long while.

'Okay, then,' he said, letting her comment slide. 'Don't stay too long.'

'Thanks, Luke.' Megan grinned as she turned to Allie. 'See. What did I tell you?'

Luke watched them go, his silent daughter walking beside his ebullient sister. It should have been the other way around—the teen with the world-weary attitude and the ten-year-old with the naïve enthusiasm.

He was failing her in some way that he couldn't understand. The things he'd tried to reach her fell dismally short of success. He was beginning to wonder if they needed a counsellor to help them through this patch. But if Allie steadfastly continued to refuse to talk, then the sessions might just cause more of a problem than they solved.

What would Terri make of his unhappy child? This week, he'd found out that she was great with children of all ages. Maybe she could see what was troubling his daughter's spirit. He would ask.

Perhaps when the girls came back he could wander down to the beach cottage.

Yeah, right. And perhaps Terri would see through him.

'She's not settling, is she?' said his father.

Allie?' Luke said, earning himself a quizzical look. 'No, she's not.'

'Maybe you should have planned a day out with her today.'

He met his parent's faintly critical gaze. 'I did. She didn't want to go.'

'Ah.' His father nodded sagely and turned his attention back to the board.

Luke contemplated the elegantly carved black and white chess pieces. White was in a hopeless position. The defence was shot and he had no offensive pieces in good positions. In short, no matter what he tried now, he was going down.

His thoughts drifted back to Allie. Every approach he'd tried had been grimly rebuffed. He'd hoped the move to Australia might have ultimately sparked some interest in her. He'd know it wouldn't be easy but he hadn't expected it to get so much worse. He had to do something soon. He couldn't stand by while his daughter sank into depression.

His father made a move, taking the white queen with his remaining knight. 'Well, maybe she needs some female company. Meggie and Terri might sort her out.'

'Maybe.' He hoped so. 'Megan's been great since we've been here.'

His father grunted. 'Wants to be a nanny. Did she tell you?'

'No, but she'd be good at it.' He castled, without much hope of salvaging his position. 'She got Allie moving, which is more than I can do these days.'

'Your mother and I have christened her the relentless angel.' There was a small pause.

Luke looked up to catch the thoughtful narrow-eyed look his father gave him over the top of his glasses.

'So, how are you finding Terri to work with? I hope you're cutting her some slack after the way the board treated her.'

'Terri doesn't need any slack to be cut from anyone, least of all me. As you well know.'

'Well, just so long as you're doing the right thing by her,' his father said gruffly. 'I don't want the hospital to lose her.'

'Neither do I.' And his concern wasn't just for the hospital.

'She's been through a lot, that girl.'

'Yes.' Luke looked back at the table. 'Has she told you what happened to her husband?'

'Just the basics. She's not much of a talker.'

'No.' So it wasn't just him that she was shutting out, thought Luke grimly.

'Hell of a tragedy, losing someone that way.'

'Yes.'

His father grunted then leaned forward to move his queen. 'Checkmate.'

'Hey. Got time for a couple of pests?'

'Always.' Terri looked up to see Megan walking around the side of the cottage. A moment later, to her surprise, Allie followed. 'Out for a walk?'

'As far as your place,' Megan said with a cheeky smile.

'I see.' Terri grinned back. 'In that case, let me finish planting the last of this punnet then I'll get us something to drink.'

'Cool,' Megan said.

Terri was aware of Allie's solemn eyes following her every move as she and Luke's sister chatted. The child was much too quiet, even allowing for natural shyness. Megan's irrepressible bubbliness wasn't succeeding in drawing her into the conversation.

'Do you like gardening, Allie?' Terri asked when there was a small silence.

Allie shrugged.

'These are herbs. When they grow bigger, I'll be able to use them for cooking.'

'Mummy has some.' Allie's toe dug into the dirt as she muttered, 'Had some.'

'Did she?' Terri patted the earth into place around the last seedling as she thought about Allie's slip and then correction. 'What did she have?'

Another shrug.

'You don't remember?'

Allie shook her head.

'When these little guys grow up, they might look more familiar.'

'I won't be here then.'

'Well, if you are. They don't take long to grow. Now, about that drink I promised.'

Terri led the way into the kitchen and went to the sink to wash her hands. When she turned, Allie was standing by the hutch. One tentative finger was stroking her old china soup tureen.

'Do you like that, Allie?'

The girl snatched her hand back, her cheeks tinting. 'Mummy's have the same pattern. I can't remember what it's called.' Her expression was infinitely sad and Terri's heart ached for her.

'It's the willow pattern. My great-great-grandmother brought a whole dinner set over to Australia with her on the ship when she came from England.'

'Same with Mummy. Not the ship. But it was from her great-, um, grandmother,' Allie said. 'I think they're pretty.'

'I think you're right.' Terri smiled and was rewarded with a tentative smile in return. She was about to ask if Allie's mother had the full set when an urgent beeping broke the moment.

Megan dug in her pocket for her phone. 'Uh-oh, it's my study partner. She wants to go over our English Lit. assignment—we're presenting it next week.'

The teen's vivid blue eyes pinned Terri with a speaking look. 'Is it okay if I leave Allie here with you?'

'Sure.'

'Thanks.' Obviously feeling that she'd delivered whatever message she'd been silently sending, Megan bounced to her feet. 'See you later, Allie cat.'

In the silence that Megan left behind, Terri and Allie eyed each other.

'I suppose you want me to go,' Allie said colourlessly.

'Stay for a bit longer if you want to.'

'Can…can I?'

'Sure. You can help me in the garden for a while. I hate seeing a willing pair of hands go unused…even an unwilling pair,' Terri teased gently.

She kept up a steady patter of information about different plants and answered Allie's occasional question. As Terri had hoped, working in the garden helped the girl to relax a little.

'There.' She sat back on her heels and looked at the garden bed they'd finished preparing. 'Haven't we done a great job?'

Allie looked at it doubtfully. 'It's just dirt.'

'Ah, yes, but it's happy dirt that's going to nourish and pamper my next crop of tomatoes which will taste extra-good. Better than anything you'll buy in a supermarket.' She smiled then glanced at her watch. 'Let me clean up and then I'll walk you home.'

'I can go by myself.' Allie sounded belligerent, ready to defend her position.

'I'm sure you can,' said Terri mildly. 'But today's

special because it's your first visit and I'd like to take you home.'

'O-okay.'

As they walked across the yard together, Terri had the impression that Allie wanted to say something. After another handful of paces, the girl finally blurted out, 'So, if this was my first visit…'

'Yes?'

'Does that mean it would be okay if I visited again? Please?'

'I don't see why not as long as it's okay with your dad.'

'It won't bother him,' she said flatly. The corners of her mouth pulled down.

'Why do you say that?'

The slender shoulders twisted into a shrug. 'Because it wouldn't.'

'I'm sure that's not true, Allie.'

Another shrug. The girl had turned the gesture into a whole new language of subtle nuances. No wonder her father was concerned. Terri felt for both of them. Allie seemed to be stuck in denial about her mother's death. Which left Luke with the sad task of helping her face the sorrow.

'Anyway, maybe I can help with your garden some more.'

'If you'd like to.' Terri smiled.

'I—I used to help Mummy sometimes.'

'Did you? Well, I'd be delighted to have you come and help me sometimes, too.'

Luke was sitting on the patio when he saw Allie and Terri come through the line of bushes. Allie was talking animatedly to Terri, much more like her old self.

And Terri was…well…Terri. Looking gorgeous in shorts cut just above the knee and battered tennis shoes. The thin knit material of her old T-shirt clung in all the right places. Her hair draped in a ponytail across one shoulder, the ends curving around her breast.

He stood, shoving his hands into his pockets, and walked across the lawn to meet them. Terri lifted her head and gave him a small smile. A moment later, Allie saw him, her face falling. He suppressed a sigh.

'Had a good time?' he said to his daughter, ignoring her sudden mood change.

'Yes. Terri said I could visit again as long as it's okay with you.' Her tone was terse. 'So may I?'

He raised one brow and his daughter's eyes slid towards Terri in a shamefaced look.

'Please?'

Luke glanced at Terri, who gave him a small nod. 'All right,' he said slowly. 'As long as you understand that Terri might have to say no sometimes.'

'Yes.'

'Okay, then.'

Her quick thanks were perfunctory but the grin she gave Terri was more open. 'Thank you, Terri.'

'Thank you for your help in the garden.' Terri smiled.

Luke cleared his throat. 'Nana's nearly ready for dinner, Allie, so how about going in to wash up?'

He watched his daughter disappear then turned to find Terri watching him, her dark eyes filled with soft sympathy. He realised abruptly that it was not the look he wanted to see when she focussed on him.

'Allie's struggling with her mother's death, isn't she?'

Shock and hope jolted through him. Had Terri managed the impossible? 'Did she talk to you?'

'Not really. I just got the impression that she hasn't accepted what's happened.'

'You're right. She hasn't. I can't seem to reach her or get her to open up at all.'

Terri looked towards the house, her face pensive. She opened her mouth as though to say something, then must have thought better of it.

'Whatever you were thinking just then…tell me,' he demanded. She gave him a startled look. 'Please,' he said, moderating his tone, 'Don't worry about offending me, just say it.'

He could see her hesitate but after a small silence, she said, 'Your daughter seems almost…angry with you.'

Conscious of a sense of disappointment, Luke slowly released the breath he'd been holding. Unreasonable though it was, he'd expected Terri's answer would provide a breakthrough for him with his daughter.

'Too true.' He gave her a wry grin.

'But it's more than that, Luke. Watching her with you just now, it's like she's made up her mind not to let you get close.' She gazed off into the distance again. 'Maybe she's punishing you for something.' Her words came haltingly, as though she was choosing each one with great care. 'Or…'

'Or?'

Her deep chocolate-brown eyes came back to his, the expression in them puzzled. 'Or maybe it's herself she's punishing.' She shook her head. 'But for what, I can't imagine.'

'Neither can I.' He silently turned over what she'd said. Perhaps there *was* an answer in her impression. He just had to find it, use it to untangle whatever was going on in Allie's mind. After a moment, he said, 'I don't know what the answer is but you've obviously worked some magic with her today.'

'Me? I haven't done anything.'

'I think you'd be surprised. It's the most enthusiasm I've seen in her for a long time so thank you.'

'Poor little girl,' she said softly as she stared in the direction that Allie had disappeared.

Luke ran his eyes over Terri's profile, taking in the thick spiky black lashes that fringed her eyes, the lovely apricot tint of her cheeks. Her lack of awareness of a tiny smudge of dirt high on her cheekbone was endearing.

Without thinking, he reached up to brush it away for her.

She jerked back, her eyes wide and alarmed. 'What are you doing?'

'You have a bit of dirt just…' He indicated on his own face as she so obviously didn't want his touch.

'Oh. Well. Thanks.' She scrubbed it as she eyed him warily. 'I, um, I'd better go, then. Bye.'

'See you tomorrow, Terri.'

'Yes, tomorrow.' She swung away. Her long easy stride carried her quickly out of his view. With a small sigh, he turned towards the house. Terri making sure Allie got home safely was laudable but now his excuse for dropping in at the cottage was gone. He smiled wryly at his disappointment.

Probably just as well.

'How are you going, Joe?' asked Terri a few days later as the patient on the bed wriggled slightly.

'Okay. Got an itch.'

'Hold still just a little longer. I'm nearly finished.' Using the dissecting forceps, she pulled back the last section of the skin flap and pushed the curved needle through the subcutaneous tissue. The needle holder made soft ratcheting clicks when she grasped the sharp tip to pull the thread through. With the final neat stitch secured, she snipped the ends and disposed of the needle in the sharps bin.

Luke wasn't on the same roster as she was today. She should have felt relief but when she tried to define her feelings, they weren't at all clear cut. If anything, she felt...flat. As though some indefinable ingredient for sparkle in the day was missing. She frowned. That nonsense needed to be stamped on quick smart.

'All done, Joe. We just need to dress that before you move.'

Joe arched his neck to look at her handiwork. 'Woah. Cool.'

'A thank you would be good, Joey,' said his mother.

'Thanks, Dr Mitchell.' The freckled face flashed a puckish grin.

'You're very welcome.'

'Terri?' Susan poked her head around the curtain. 'We've got a ten-year-old with ARD on the way in.'

'Okay. Thanks, Susan. I'm just finishing up here.'

An odd look crossed Susan's face as she hesitated a second. 'Shall I send someone in to dress that for you?'

'Okay. And a tetanus booster, too, thanks.' Something was definitely worrying the nurse. She stripped off the gloves and said to her delighted patient, 'You'll need to keep the dressing on and dry for twenty-four hours and we'll see you back here in a week to have the stitches removed.'

'Okay.'

'The wound was very clean,' she said to Joe's mother.

'But if you have any concerns, don't hesitate to come back and see us.'

'Thanks, Terri.'

'Someone will be here in a minute to put a dressing on that and give you a sheet of instructions.' Terri smiled and excused herself.

She found Susan in the office, making a note on the patient tracking board.

'Problem?' Terri said.

'Maybe.' Susan looked up, frowning. 'The message was a bit confused but I think the ARD patient is Luke's daughter.'

Terri's hands stilled. 'What makes you think that?'

'The teacher who called it in was very shaken but she kept saying it was Alexis and asking for Dr Daniels.'

'Ambulance dispatched?' Terri swallowed a stab of foreboding. Luke had mentioned Allie's worsening asthma attacks.

'No. The child was already in transit with one of the other teachers when the call was made.'

'Right, what's their ETA?'

'Now. The class was on a field trip to the museum. They decided to make the dash straight here rather than wait for an ambulance as they're only a couple of blocks away.'

Terri suppressed a sigh. She could understand the temptation to make the dash, but it was precious minutes that the child should have been having treatment.

'Okay. I agree, let's assume that it is Alexis. Have we got medical records for her?'

'I've rung Admin,' said Susan. 'They're on the way.'

'Great. Thanks.' Terri glanced at the clock. Ten o'clock. She wondered what Luke had planned. He wouldn't be too far away because he was on duty this evening. She didn't want to page him unnecessarily but she knew he'd want to be there if it was Allie having the attack.

'Let's confirm the identity of our patient...' She trailed off as a car drove into the emergency drop-off point and the sliding doors swished open. The child in the passenger's seat was hunched forward so that she couldn't see a face. But the bob of straight dark hair looked all too familiar.

Her stomach swooped.

'Call Luke, stat, please, Susan,' she called, picking up an oxygen cylinder and mask as she raced for the door.

CHAPTER SIX

'OH, DOCTOR, thank goodness,' gasped the young pale woman rushing around the car to intersect with Terri at the passenger door. 'The attack's so bad. I didn't think we were going to make it.'

Terri leaned into the car, conscious of the teacher hovering behind her as she ran a critical eye over Allie. Hunched shoulders, hands pressed to her sides as she laboured for breath, audibly wheezing with each hard-won lungful.

'Hi, Allie. Can you understand me?'

The glossy head gave a tiny nod.

'I'm going to put an oxygen mask on you.' She fitted the soft plastic mask over the blue-tinged lips and flaring nostrils. Frightened blue eyes clung to hers briefly before closing.

'I've got a gurney here, Terri,' said Susan.

'Okay, let's get her inside.'

Terri was shocked by how frail the child felt in her arms. She settled her on the gurney, seating her as upright as possible.

Susan wheeled the gurney through to a cubicle as Terri took a set of obs. Allie's slender shoulders rose and fell at a rate of about forty respirations per minute. Beneath her fingertips, Terri could feel the child's radial pulse rocketing at one hundred and sixty beats per minute.

'I know it's hard, sweetheart, but I want you to try to relax as much as you can, slow down your breathing.' Terri clipped a pulse oximeter onto one dainty finger.

Another slow nod.

'We're looking after you now and we'll have you comfortable in no time,' she said soothingly.

'Where's Daddy?'

'He's on his way, sweetheart. Susan's taking your shirt off now so she can attach some dots to your skin.'

With the clothing stripped away, Terri could see the way each desperate breath hollowed out the soft tissues around Allie's clavicle, leaving skin gleaming white over angular bone.

Terri placed the stethoscope diaphragm on Allie's chest and listened to pounding heartbeats accompanying the harsh wheeze in the girl's lungs. No sound at all would have been a very bad sign.

'Do you think you could do a peak flow for me?'

The dark head bobbed and Allie reached for the tube.

'Good girl.' Terri glanced at the scale on the side of the tube. The baseline reading was forty percent of what she'd expect for a child of Allie's age and size. 'Allie, have you been taking preventative medication?'

'Didn't. Take.'

'What about your puffer, sweetheart? Did you have it with you at the museum today?'

The cubicle curtain clattered and suddenly Luke was beside the gurney.

Allie raised shadowed eyes to her father then looked at Terri and shook her head tiredly.

'Okay, sweetie,' Terri said. 'Susan, a gown, large, and a pair of gloves, please.'

'Allie, honey, what happened?' Luke stroked the hair off her forehead with hands that shook visibly. 'Try to relax, sweetheart.' He looked up at the oximeter and then pinned Terri with a fierce look. 'What's going on? Her oxygen sat is only eighty-nine per cent. Why isn't she on a nebuliser?'

'We're just about to start one,' Terri said gently. 'Luke, you have to let us do our job. Your job is to be calm for Allie.'

His face worked as he pulled himself back under control. When he spoke, his voice was rough but more measured. 'I'm staying.'

'I know. Susan's beside you with a gown and gloves for you. So, let's get this nebuliser started.' She was aware of him moving, pulling on the gown, as she broke an ampule of bronchodilator into the nebuliser cup. Oxygen gurgled noisily through the liquid, delivering a fine mist of life-saving bronchodilator. The clear plastic frosted with Allie's urgent rasping breaths.

Terri glanced at Luke. How hard it must be for him to see Allie's battle. His strong features reflected the suffering his daughter was going through. The naked emotion brought a hot lump to her throat.

She turned away to check Allie's readings.

Little response. She prepared a second inhalation and bent to swap the nebuliser cup. 'Do you think you could swallow something for me, Allie?'

The girl nodded.

'Have you got a favourite jam?'

Another nod.

'Apricot?' The dark head shook.

'Strawberry,' Luke said, his voice hoarse. A nod from Allie.

'Susan, could you mash prednisolone in jam, please? We're going with the strawberry.'

Luke watched Terri smile at his daughter. He could see the situation was desperate. As a father he wanted to yell and rage and demand she do something to help Allie, to relieve his daughter's suffering, to make it better.

Stat!

As a doctor, he knew everything that could be done was being done.

Thank God for Terri. Calm, competent, caring. Confidence-inspiring. He was grateful for the small tasks she assigned him. He was there to be with his daughter, that's what mattered. It helped him that he was doing something, no matter how small.

Three hours later, Terri opened the door to Allie's room and tiptoed across to the bed where Luke sat keeping watch. They'd worked for two hours to stabilise Allie. He'd been ready to slay monsters to save her if necessary. His protective concern appealed deeply and Terri realised she felt acutely vulnerable having seen him this way.

Only now that the frightening attack was over could she admit how serious the situation had been. The thought that she might have failed Luke, failed Allie, sent a shaft of nausea into her stomach.

She touched Luke's shoulder. He stirred, turning to look up at her. His expression was dazed.

'She's going to be okay now.'

'Yes, thanks to you.'

'Thanks to the team.' She looked at his drawn face, lines of exhaustion etched around his mouth, and her heart squeezed. 'Take a break, get something to eat and drink, Luke.'

He opened his mouth, refusal in his eyes.

'Just for a few minutes. I'll stay here with Allie.'

She could see he still wanted to refuse.

'I promise I'll be right here when you get back.'

'Okay.' He stood slowly and arched his back. 'Thank you. I won't be long.'

'I know.' She smiled.

Alone with Allie, Terri smoothed the sheet at the edge of the bed and allowed herself a moment longer to watch the sleeping child. It was a pleasure and a relief to see the steady respirations and better skin colour. To check the monitor and see pulse, oxygen saturation and respiratory rate all nearly within the normal range. A stark contrast to the girl who had presented in the emergency department.

For the initial one hundred minutes of her admission, it had been all too possible that her condition could have deteriorated disastrously. She'd been so tired, using accessory muscles as she'd fought for breath.

Terri stroked Allie's forehead, watching the fragile eyelids flutter open above the oxygen mask. Blue eyes, startlingly like her father's, flickered and focussed slowly.

'Hey, sweetheart,' Terri said softly. 'How are you feeling?'

'Okay.' Allie smiled weakly. Her pale skin contrasted with the purple-grey crescents that shadowed her eyes.

As her eyes cleared, she looked around.

'Your dad will be back in a minute,' said Terri. 'He's been sitting with you since you came in.'

'I know. I don't know why,' she said, her voice filled with pain as she closed her eyes and turned her head away.

Terri blinked and stood lost for words for a long moment. 'What do you mean, Allie?'

The girl's mouth trembled. 'H-he hates me.'

'Oh, honey—' Denial sprang to Terri's lips, her tongue started to form the words. She stopped, stifling the automatic response. Allie believed what she was saying.

'Can you tell me why you think that?'

Allie flicked her silent sideways glance, her eyes tortured beneath the lake of brimming tears.

'Your dad's very worried about you,' Terri said softly. 'He loves you very much and he wants to help you. I think he's sad because he doesn't know how. Maybe if you talked to him—'

'You don't understand.' The soft tortured words were ripped from a deep anguished place and tears spilled over to stream down Allie's cheeks. 'I don't deserve to be happy.'

'Oh, Allie.' Terri reached for the slender shoulders, drawing the crying girl into an embrace. 'Tell me what you mean, sweetheart.'

Terri rocked her gently and waited.

'D-Dad was w-with me when Mummy died. It's m-my fault.'

'Oh, sweetheart,' Terri murmured as she rubbed the girl's back and listened to the story of guilt and anger and unresolved grief that tumbled out. Interspersed with sobs and hiccups, it wasn't easy to understand, but she didn't interrupt the flow. Finally, Allie wound down.

'It's not your fault that your mum died.' Terri squeezed her gently, her heart swelling when Allie's arms crept around her waist and clung. 'You're grieving and your thoughts are all jumbled up, aren't they?'

'It f-feels bad.'

'I know, sweetheart. I know.' She stroked the girl's hair and pressed her lips to the top of her head. 'Have you tried to talk to your dad about this at all?'

'No,' came the whispered response. 'I can't tell him.'

'He'll understand, Allie.'

'He'll be angry.'

'Never. He might be sad for not seeing why you've been so unhappy. But he'd never be angry with you for the way you're feeling now.'

Eyes framed by spiky drenched lashes lifted to cling to hers. Panic and a tiny growing spark of hope swam in the blue depths.

'Your dad will be back in a few minutes. What say we tell him together then?''

'Y-you'll help?'

'Of course. In the meantime, how about I check you over? Sit forward for me so I can listen to your chest.' Terri recorded Allie's obs while she kept up a steady stream of chatter and questions to keep the girl's mind occupied.

Terri knew the moment Luke slipped quietly into the room. All her senses quivered with awareness. 'Here's your dad now.'

Allie's smile dimmed and Terri suppressed a sigh. She waited until Luke was standing on the other side of the bed. 'Allie told me some things she's been worrying about, Luke. She's going to be very brave and tell you about them.'

'Allie, that's great, sweetheart,' he said softly.

'Allie?' Terri prompted after a pause.

The girl plucked at the sheet, her eyes averted. Luke's eyes filled with baffled hunger as they settled on his daughter.

The silence felt thick with accusation. Terri's stomach clenched painfully. In her eagerness to help, had she made a monumental error? Would professional counselling have been the wiser course?

But she was so sure they didn't need an intermediary; they just needed to start. Terri bit her lip as she debated what to do next. Her instincts told her it would be better if Allie could tell her father herself. Much more therapeutic. But perhaps the stress was too much for the child.

'Allie, darling... I know you're unhappy.' Luke's voice was gentle and coaxing. 'I know it's not easy but I want you to know that you can tell me anything, anything at all. I won't be cross with you.'

Terri's throat blocked with tears and pride for the man as he tried to connect with his daughter. His words were just right. So honest and brave and perceptive. No defences. No armour. He'd lost people close to him and yet he was still prepared to put his feelings on the line for those he loved.

Perhaps this was a lesson she needed to learn. She'd thought she'd lost her physical courage in the landmine explosion. But maybe she'd never had what really counted— the raw emotional courage she was witnessing now between father and daughter.

Allie's head stayed bowed, her shoulders rounded.

Luke's eyes were soft with hope and love. 'I promise I'll listen and between us we'll try to find a compromise.'

There was a long tense silence. Terri held her breath and willed Allie to answer.

Luke glanced up and she gave him a tiny nod of encouragement. His throat moved as he swallowed, then he looked back at the top of his daughter's head.

'And even if I can't make it better,' he said, 'I will always love you, Allie.'

'How can you?' The girl sucked in a slightly wheezy breath, her arms wrapping tightly around her thin body. Terri's heart ached at the sight of the defensive movement.

Then, in a tiny, unsteady voice, the girl said, 'Mummy died because of me.'

'No!' The last vestige of colour drained from Luke's face. He laid his arm on Allie's shoulder. 'No, baby.'

'Yes!' she whispered.

'Oh, Allie.' His face twisted. 'Why, sweetheart? Why do you think that?'

'You could have fixed her b-but you were looking after me so she d-died.' Tears streamed down Allie's flushed cheeks and her words came out haltingly between spasmodic sobs. 'She'd still be alive if it w-wasn't for me.'

'No, Allie. I'm sorry.' Luke could hardly get the words out through the constriction in his throat. Why hadn't he intuitively understood the cause of his daughter's anguish? He was her father, for God's sake. 'I wouldn't have been able to fix your mum.'

'B-but I get sick,' she said. 'You always f-fix me.'

'Sweetheart, your mum's sickness was different. The cells in her blood multiplied and multiplied and we couldn't find a way to stop them.' He sat on the edge of her bed, wanting to gather her into his arms but not wanting to push while she was so defensive. 'I'm sorry, Allie. I didn't realise you were feeling this way. I let you down.'

'No.' With a choked cry, Allie suddenly launched herself at him. He hugged her close, her thin arms wrapped around his neck tightly. The frail body against his shook with great sobbing shudders.

He breathed deep. His child, his baby, had thrown herself into his arms. The stamp of this small person's scent affixed itself on his soul all over again.

It had all been made possible by one extraordinary woman.

He lifted his head in time to see Terri swiping her hands across her cheeks as she turned to leave.

'Terri?'

She hesitated a moment then lifted brimming eyes to meet his. His chest swelled at the unsteady smile she gave him. He owed this woman more than he could ever repay. He wished he could reach out and draw her into the circle of his embrace with Allie.

'Thank you,' he murmured.

She nodded, nudging a box of tissues along the bed-side dresser until it was within easy reach for him. 'I'll let the switchboard know that I'm taking your calls until further notice.'

His heart was full as he watched her slip out of the room, shutting the door behind her.

He held Allie until her sobs subsided. In a small silence he grabbed a couple of tissues and proffered them.

'Thanks.' She blew her nose with unselfconscious vigour, then sighed. After a moment, she said, 'I miss Mummy.'

The wobble in her voice tore at his heart.

'I do, too, Allie.'

'We left her.'

He frowned. 'When we came here?'

'Yes. W-we left her behind.' She tilted her head to look at him. 'We left all the places she loved.'

'She loved it here, too,' he said. With his thumb, he wiped the moisture from her cheeks. 'Remember last time we were here together? She taught you how to snorkel.'

'Yes. But it's not the same.' Her voice was thick with unshed tears. 'We left her garden.'

'I know, baby, I know.' Luke understood immediately. The garden had been Sue-Ellen's pride and joy. She'd lavished love on her plants with the same generosity she'd lavished it on her family. He swallowed as a quick stab of grief pierced his heart. 'You know Mr Owens is looking after it for us.' He laid his cheek on the top of her head. 'But it's not the same as us being there, is it?'

Allie's hair rubbed his skin as she nodded. 'He won't love it as much as w-we would.' Her voice shook anew.

'I know.' He gave her a quick tight squeeze. The silence was comfortable, soothing. He rubbed her back in slow circles, enjoying the closeness after so many months of friction.

'T-Terri said maybe we could get a plant.'

'To remember your mum by? Would you like that?' How brilliant. How elegantly simple. Bless Terri and her insight.

Allie's head, cuddled against his chest, nodded.

'I think that's a great idea. We can go to the nursery and you can pick something out.'

'I already know what I want to get. A pink rose like the one we had by the front door.' She lifted her eyes to his, the lashes spiky with tears. 'The climbing one.'

'Okay. We'll get the very best pink climbing rose in the nursery.'

Allie rewarded him with a radiant smile, a glimpse of the healing process that had begun. The moment was precious. 'Can Terri come, too? When we get it?'

Luke quelled a pinprick of apprehension. *Terri*. Both he and Allie wanted more of her in their lives. It seemed like a potential disaster. He didn't want Allie to get hurt.

For him the want, the *need*, was on a very different level. In an instant of uncomfortable clarity he realised he was projecting his fears for himself onto his daughter.

He didn't want to get hurt. Didn't want to risk losing

someone else that he cared about. Didn't want to put his heart on the line.

He stifled a sigh. He was afraid that his options for choice in the matter were well gone.

'Can she, Dad?'

'Of course. If she wants to.' He shook off the shiver of disturbing self-awareness. A family outing with Terri might help to take the magic out of her presence, give him a bit of perspective where she was concerned. 'We'll talk to your granddad, too, and see where we can put the rose.'

'Somewhere special.'

'Somewhere extra-special.'

'Thanks, Dad.' She reached up and hugged him spontaneously again. The lump in his throat got bigger. 'I feel better.'

'So do I, Allie. So do I.'

He had his daughter back. Right now, this was what counted. Allie relied on him to make sensible choices.

For her and for him.

A short time later, Terri filled out a biochemistry form requesting urea and electrolytes and slipped it into a laboratory collection bag with a tube of blood.

As soon as she'd finished, her mind strayed towards the room at the end of the emergency department where Allie had been moved once she'd been stabilised. How were Luke and his daughter? When Terri had left them half an hour ago, Luke had had his hip perched on the edge of the bed and Allie wrapped in his arms.

A cocoon of paternal protection.

A beautiful snapshot of love between parent and child.

Terri swallowed. What sort of parents would she and Peter have been? Her hand ran down the flatness of her abdomen. She already knew he'd had no time for her pregnancy. The changes in her body, which had so delighted her, had left her late husband cold. She tried to imagine him enfolding a child, their child, in his arms.

That picture wouldn't come.

Suddenly she needed to see Luke with Allie, to see that affirmation of pure, unconditional love. Her feet carried her past the curtained cubicles to the door of Allie's room.

There they were. She rested her fingertips lightly on the glass of the window and felt the tension in her chest ease.

They were going to be okay, this father and daughter who had each carved a niche in her heart.

As she watched, Allie's arms came up to wrap around Luke's neck. The scene in the room blurred. Terri lifted her hands, pressed her fingers to her eyelids as she willed away the unexpected rush of moisture.

The moment between parent and child was infinitely precious. They'd been through some very tough times, but they would get through it together and be even closer on the other side.

As though he'd felt her presence, Luke's head lifted and looked straight at her. Her pulse gave a treacherous leap.

He smiled crookedly, tilted his head in an invitation to join them.

Terri swallowed then opened the door.

'Hi,' she said softly. Her smile felt wobbly.

'We've got something to ask you, haven't we, Allie?' Luke's voice was husky.

'Yes.' Allie grinned. Her cheeks were tinged with pink and the strain had faded from her eyes. She looked like a normal happy ten-year-old. 'Please, will you come to the nursery with us when we chose the plant for Mummy? Please say you will. Please.'

'Of course. I'd be honoured. When's the big day or haven't you got that far in the planning yet?'

'There's no school tomorrow.'

'I think Sunday week perhaps.' Luke touched his daughter on the nose. 'Terri and I are rostered off then and it'll give your granddad a chance to decide where he wants the garden.'

Terri blinked in surprise. He knew her roster that far ahead? She stifled a foolish glow of warmth. He probably knew everyone's shifts—it wasn't as if they had a huge medical staff.

'Sunday week, then,' she said.

Luke smiled. 'We'll let you know what time.'

'Okay.' She slid her hands into the pockets of her coat. 'I'd better get back to work. I just wanted to look in and see how you were.'

'We're good. Aren't we, Dad?'

'We are indeed.' His eyes were filled with light and warmth and something more. Something that made Terri's heart lurch. 'I'll catch up with you before you go off duty, Terri.'

'Sure,' she managed. 'I'm off at five, all being well.'

'I know.' His slow smile sent a hot shaft of excitement sizzling along her diaphragm.

'It's a pleasure, Edith,' Terri said as she opened the door to let her last patient out. 'Keep off that foot as much as possible and we'll see you again next week.'

'Next Friday. Thanks again, dear.' Leaning heavily on her walking frame, the woman hobbled a couple of steps then stopped in the doorway. 'Oh, Luke. How are you?'

'Good, thanks, Edith.' His smile seemed tense to Terri's eye but he stopped to exchanged pleasantries with the elderly woman. 'If you'll excuse me, I need an urgent word with Terri, with Dr Mitchell.'

'Of course, dear. We'll chat another time.'

'Absolutely.' He nodded. A muscle rippled in his jaw as though he was keeping his emotions on a tight leash while he chatted with Edith. He stood aside so she could move through the door. 'You can count on it.'

As soon as the patient had gone, he shut the door. The latch snicked loudly in the silence and he stood for a moment with his hand on the doorknob.

Terri's mouth went dry. 'Luke. Is there a problem with Allie?'

'No. No. Just the opposite.' His voice was gruff as he turned.

Terri found herself scooped into a tight hug. For a split second she froze as sensations tumbled into her brain. The feeling of his solid body aligned with hers, the heat and strength of his arms wrapped around her. The fresh essence of him, faintly tangy, masculine and clean. She flattened her hands on his back, feeling the hard ridge of muscle on either side of his spine.

She shut her eyes, savouring the contact as her knees turned rubbery. The embrace felt wonderful and for a magical instant his touch erased her sorrow and filled empty places in her spirit. In his arms, she felt more whole than she had for a long, long time.

After a moment, he held her at arm's length, his eyes burning down into hers.

'Thank you.' His throat worked as he struggled to speak. 'I owe you more than I can ever repay.'

'Oh, Luke.' This glimpse into his vulnerability was wrenching. Terri ached for him. She reached up to cup his cheek.

He brought his hand up, held her fingers more firmly to his face. The very faint roughness of his clean-shaven jaw tingled on her skin. Her heart squeezed.

'You saved my daughter's life and you've performed a miracle by getting her talking to me.' His head dipped and his lips touched her palm for a tiny thrilling moment.

She sucked in a quick breath at the caress, reminding herself that it meant nothing. Luke was naturally demonstrative and this moment was an emotional one for him. His love for his daughter and his relief at their reunion was spilling over into his actions. But her stubborn heart somersaulted wildly, refusing to listen to common sense.

'You've given her back to me, Terri.'

With her senses so overloaded with physical awareness, she struggled to bring her mind back to their discussion. *Allie.* 'You never lost her, Luke. She loves you very much. You know she does. She's just confused right now. You were the person she asked for when she was brought in today.'

'Was I? Thank you.' His grip tightened on her hand briefly when she tried to withdraw her fingers. After a moment he released her and a grin lit up his face. 'She hugged me.'

'Yeah, she did.' Terri's smile felt quivery. 'I saw.'

He sobered. 'My poor baby. Thinking her mother's death was her fault. I didn't see it. I still don't know how she could have believed it.'

'Children have their own view of the way the world works.' She curled her fingers into her palm, as though by holding tight she could lock the sensory memory of his skin on hers. Maybe part of the reason she had been able to tap into Allie's feelings was because of her hyper-sensitivity to the girl's father. 'They sometimes feel responsible for things in a way that an adult wouldn't consider.'

'Yes.' He paced away from her, lifting one hand to his forehead. His fingers furrowed through his hair, leaving endearing tufts standing in their wake.

Terri allowed her gaze to stray over his broad shoulders. The soft woven fabric of his white shirt showed off his powerful torso to perfection. With the sleeves rolled up to elbow level, she could appreciate his muscular forearms. She smiled wryly. She'd always had a weakness for nice arms and hands.

And firm thighs and posteriors. She sighed. The navy denim of Luke's jeans fitted him very well indeed.

He spun around and his eyes drilled into hers. Heat crawled into her face as though she'd been caught doing something she shouldn't.

'No wonder I couldn't reach her. I should have listened to you the other day when you suggested she was punishing herself.' He moved restlessly to the side again and Terri released the breath caught in her lungs. 'She was so ill. I can't get the picture of her struggling for breath out of my mind.'

'Luke—'

He looked back at her fiercely. 'I nearly lost it in the emergency room.'

'But you didn't.'

'Only thanks to you treating me like a raw intern.'

'Allie is your daughter. Of course it was difficult for you.'

'I don't know what I'd have done if—'

'Stop this. Right now.' She knew too well how he'd have felt. She might not be a parent in the full sense of the word but she knew what it was like to lose a child. The guilt could be paralysing. 'Stop torturing yourself. Allie has recovered and she needs her father. All of him. Not someone fractured by guilt. It's a pointless emotion when you should be concentrating on each other.'

'Yes. You're right.' He dragged a hand down his face then gave her a gorgeous, lopsided smile. 'Thank you. For everything. Including the pep talk. You see things beyond the physical. It makes you an extraordinary doctor, Terri.'

Terri swallowed and looked away. She shoved her hands into her coat pockets. His praise was almost more than she could bear because she knew exactly how limited her abilities were.

He trusted her.

It was priceless.

It was an almost intolerable burden.

She wanted to warn him not to think too highly of her. Warn him how very flawed her judgement could be.

'Luke, please…' Her voice was croaky. She cleared her throat before continuing. 'I was just doing—'

'Don't say you were just doing your job. It was much more than that. We're lucky to have you here at Port Cavill.' He looked deeply into her eyes and there was no doubting his sincerity. '*I'm* lucky to have you here.'

The warm approval was too much. She needed to shrug it off, find a way to keep him at a distance, to quash this intimacy that seemed to have sprung up between them.

'Well,' she said, struggling for a light note, 'I'm glad you think so. Please remember this when I do something to blot my copy book.'

Her smile felt ghastly as she blinked back the urge to cry. She needed to go, find somewhere private to pull herself back together. She cast unseeing eyes in the direction of her watch and said, 'I must catch the lab tech before she goes for the day.'

She all but fled, not caring what he thought. As the

barrier of the door clicked shut behind her, she sagged with relief.

Too much, too soon. Being close to him showed her how very flimsy the shell of her carefully mended persona was. She wasn't ready for the powerful, conflicting emotions that Luke awakened. She wondered if she ever would be. She shivered. How long would she be able to hold the façade together under the pressure?

Luke stared at the door after Terri had gone.

He frowned. She'd seemed embarrassed by his thanks. More than that, she'd seemed ashamed, as though she was somehow undeserving of them. But that was ridiculous— she'd saved his daughter's life today.

He'd been there, he'd seen how hard she'd worked, seen her skill and determination. He couldn't praise her highly enough for what she'd done.

He owed her. He respected her.

And he wanted her.

Needy hunger that clawed at him. He'd held her in his arms twice now—embraces that had started out with the very best platonic intentions. But he'd felt the heat grow in his lower abdomen on both occasions, giving the contact with her a sizzling, inappropriate energy.

Familiarity wasn't kicking in as quickly as he'd hoped. He just had to keep holding himself in check until it did.

He huffed out a breath. An armful of Terri Mitchell would test the restraint of a saint. All he had was the very tenuous control of Luke Daniels and it was no match for the temptation of her.

CHAPTER SEVEN

LUKE pushed open his car door and stood listening to the high pitched howl of hard-working motorcycle engines.

He was escaping. Just for the day.

At his mother's behest, he'd left Allie with her for a girls' day out. Shopping. His daughter was really excited about it. He smiled wryly, hard pressed to think of anything he'd like to do less.

He was also escaping from the lure of Terri. She had the day off but he had no good excuse to invade his colleague's off-duty hours. Other than the fact that he wanted to.

With Allie gone for the day, he couldn't casually suggest a walk on the beach…via Terri's cottage on the off chance that she was around. Having her so close, at the bottom of the garden, was a refined form of torture.

He sighed. Rather than hang around home testing his self-discipline, he was going to face a personal demon. He'd loved hanging out at the racetrack with his cousin Kevin, and Terri's brother Ryan. He hadn't been back since Kevin's accident.

Hadn't been on a bike either. But that was something to tackle another day…perhaps. For now, being here was an accomplishment.

He'd talk to Mick Butler while he was here, too. An informal follow-up after the diabetic episode. He smiled wryly. Maybe he would earn himself some Brownie points with Terri.

He walked through the tunnel under the track to the pit area and watched the speeding bikes for a few moments. Just an initial tightening in his chest, he noted dispassionately. Nothing unmanageable.

He took a deep breath and looked at the people standing trackside. His lips curved when he spotted a familiar profile. Terri's uncle.

'G'day, Mick!'

The man turned. 'Luke Daniels!'

Their palms smacked together as they used the handshake to draw into a quick, hard embrace of uncomplicated masculine friendship.

Mick stood back, his wide smile and dark eyes familiar and uncannily like Terri's. 'About time you showed your face around here!'

'Yeah, I know.' Luke shrugged. 'Time gets away. You know how it is.'

'I know.' Mick patted his arm, the gesture awkward but the emotion behind it genuine. 'I was sorry to hear about Sue-Ellen. She was a bonzer girl.'

Luke nodded. 'Yes, she was. Thanks. I got your card.'

'How's that gorgeous daughter of yours?'

'Giving me grey hairs.' Luke smiled.

'It gets worse.' Mick chuckled. 'I remember when my girls—'

He was interrupted by loud whoops and clapping from the men nearest them. Mick's head whipped back to the course.

'She's just taken Russ,' called one of the appreciative audience. 'Boy, he's going to be dirty about that.'

'She?' A corkscrew of unease twisted through Luke's gut. No, it couldn't be…could it?

'Terri.' Mick craned his neck, following the action. 'She's on the yellow Honda.'

Luke's heart leapt into his throat. His eyes followed the motorcycle as it tipped into another sweeping bend in a blur of red leather and yellow bike.

'That's Terri?'

Terri! Oh, God.

Desire and fear congealed into a solid lump of cold ice in his gut.

Leaning, leaning… Surely the bike must slide from under her. That long crouching form would be thrown, fragile bones crushed, gentle curves mutilated.

How dared she risk her precious life like this?

The woman. Was going. To drive him. Insane.

'Yeah, good, isn't she? Could've gone pro if she hadn't been so set on medicine.' Obviously unconcerned, Terri's uncle turned away as one of the other riders came in.

Good?

Good!

Luke wanted to demand that she be called off the track, stat. He folded his arms, feeling the tightness pinch around his eyes and mouth. Acid churned in his stomach. He'd been watching the speeding riders with reasonable detachment, congratulating himself for managing that degree of calm. The accident which had killed his cousin had been years ago. Past time for him to let go his visceral antipathy to motorcycles.

But now…

Now he knew it was Terri on the track, he felt sick.

And angry.

Angrier by the minute.

Two circuits later, she slowed and pulled into the pit area. Oblivious to his glowering presence, she stopped to chat briefly to a couple of the mechanics further along the lane. Her long legs braced on either side of the machine. With a quick nod, she rode forward slowly. The machine's throaty growl sounded a protest at the restrained speed as she turned into the empty garage.

Luke stalked across the tarmac, driven by the desire to give her a verbal blast. He turned into the wide door. Terri stood beside the bike, stripping off her gloves.

The skin-tight red leather suit moulded to her lithe body.

His gaze was drawn irresistibly down over each feminine curve.

Breast, waist, hip, thigh.

At the knee, the bright supple covering disappeared into long black boots.

Luke swallowed, his steps slowing as an unexpected shudder shook him.

His eyes made the return trip.

She was gorgeous, sensual.

Dangerous to his sanity.

As he watched, she unclipped her helmet and shook out waves of long dark hair.

Perfection.

And she would risk it all for a thrill, a momentary pleasure.

His daughter had made a confidante of this reckless creature. Allie wouldn't be able to cope with another flood of grief in her young life. Terri needed to consider that when she indulged her whim for danger.

Bubbling anger dimmed a tiny internal alarm that

sounded in his brain. *Walk away. Don't do this, don't do this. Walk away, now.*

His entire system twitched with the need for an argument, even relished the prospect in a perverse way.

His feet moved purposefully until he was only a few feet from her. She turned. The radiant smile on her lips tilted higher. He could see the high of exhilaration was still pumping through her system.

'Hi, Luke.' Her buoyant greeting was the last straw.

'I suppose you're proud of that display out there,' he said softly.

She tipped her head slightly to one side. 'The riding?'

'Yes, the riding,' he grated.

'Oh, yes. I suppose I am a bit. Did you see?' She still hadn't realised his dangerous state of mind. Enthusiasm shone through her voice. She stuffed her gloves into the hollow of the helmet and then stood with it dangling from one hand.

'I saw,' he said grimly. 'What sort of example do you think you're setting?'

'Example? Well…a good one, I hope. I was in absolute control of the bike at all times,' she said, her voice confused.

'All it takes is a loss of concentration for a split second.' He ground his teeth together. The muscle tension in his jaw was painful. 'People rely on you. Patients up at the hospital. My family. My daughter.'

And me. What about me? How am I going to feel if your broken body ends up in Accident and Emergency? He managed to clamp his mouth shut before the telling words escaped.

'You have a responsibility to this community.' He sounded foolish but, even realising that, he was powerless to stop himself.

'Luke, I—'

'What if something happened to you?'

She gave him a long, searching look. Her expression melted into a look of profound compassion. 'Oh, I'm so sorry. This is about Kevin, isn't it? How insensitive of me. I know it was hard for you, the way he died, but you can't hold onto that grief, Luke. For your sake and for Allie's, it's time to let it go.'

He swore a brief, earthy oath. 'You think this is about Kevin?'

'Well, yes.' Her beautiful face was uncertain and he could see her trying to read his mood. 'Isn't it?'

'No. God damn it. This is about *you*, Terri.'

She took a step back, retreating from the fierceness he knew he was radiating.

'I—I think you need to calm down and then maybe we can talk about this. Perhaps later.' She pivoted and started to walk past him. 'For now, I—'

Without thinking, he reached out, snagging her elbow. The force of her momentum spun her around and landed her hard on his chest, one hand braced at his waist. His fingers flexed around her upper arms where he'd reached out to steady her. Her well-worn leathers felt warm and soft, oddly intimate against his palms.

He gulped in a lungful of air, starting the move to set her back on her feet.

Then she lifted her head. Her lips trembled only inches from his and all his good intentions evaporated.

'Terri.' His voice, so ragged, sounded shockingly needy, desperate.

'Luke.' His name was little more than a whisper.

Dark, nearly black eyes held his for a long moment before slipping, heavy-lidded, to his mouth. Instead of freeing her, he pulled her closer, tilted his head, slanted his lips over the fullness of hers.

No awkwardness, no hesitation. The delight of unexpected familiarity mingled with the wonder and excitement of discovery. She made a small humming sound, almost a moan.

The hand at his waist relaxed, then tightened again before creeping around his back as she pressed into him. The pressure of each fingertip burned through the thin fabric of his shirt. He revelled in the touch, wanted more, wanted it on his skin.

All his anger with her carelessness, his fear for her safety, everything, drained away. Her lips parted in a sweet moist caress, so soft and mobile. Delicious.

A thrill streaked through him, blotting out coherent thought, reducing his world to the sensation of her body pressed to his. She made him want to give more—take more—than was sensible.

A single resonating crunch ripped through the moment. Terri's head jerked back, her torso arching away from his. She stared up at him, eyes wide and stunned. As he watched, the dazed expression cleared from her eyes. Her hands, which had been clasped across his back, now flattened on his chest as she shoved herself away from him.

He swallowed. His system was revved, heart pumping, muscles ready to take on dragons.

The only thing he wasn't ready for was Terri. She looked utterly shattered. Her breasts rose and fell shakily with each shallow, rapid breath.

The helmet, the source of the noise, rocked back and forth on the floor beside them.

Terri started to raise her hand to her face and he saw the tremor in her fingers. As though she suddenly realised what she was doing, her fingers closed in a fist that was pulled sharply back to her side.

'What did you do that for?'

'I'm sorry.' His voice was hoarse, the words meaningless. He wasn't sorry. Not at all. Given the option this moment, he'd take up where they'd left off.

'You're s-sorry?' Her voice rose and she looked momentarily as shocked as he was by the note of hysteria. She glowered at him. Then her face slowly crumpled.

'Oh, God. What have you done? I was okay when I though it was just m...' she trailed off, her expression appalled.

'Just you?' His heart bumped. She felt the same way he did.

She stiffened, pulling herself together before his eyes. 'Just... This thing... Us... We can't...' She touched her forehead with her fingers, rubbing hard at the skin. 'Oh, what am I saying? There is no us. We're colleagues. Nothing more. Do you hear me?' She looked up at him then, the expression in her eyes desperate, daring him to disagree.

She was wrong. Though he couldn't point that out. Not right now.

Not when he could see how devastated she was.

Not when his own system was shaking and shuddering in the aftermath of the kiss.

He didn't understand what was behind her reaction but he needed to find a way to soothe her. He lifted a hand to reach out, make a tiny physical connection...

She nearly leapt away from him.

'Terri—'

'I have to go.'

He watched her long legs powering her away from him, agitation clear in every rapid step.

She didn't want anything more than a professional relationship, that much was clear. But it didn't alter the fact that she'd kissed him back.

Wildly.

Wantonly.

He felt like a teenager, giddy and stupid after the voluptuousness of his first kiss.

And it was a first...his first passionate kiss since his wife had died. He scrubbed his hands down his face. Why had he done it? He hadn't felt as though he had a choice—once she had been in his arms, blind instinct had taken over. For both of them.

He didn't want to think about replacing his wife. He wasn't ready.

Was he?

He could almost feel his reality shifting around him. He swallowed. Maybe he was ready.

Kissing Terri didn't feel like the betrayal he'd have predicted if there'd been time to consider before acting.

Quite simply, the kiss was the most important thing to have happened to him, as a man, for two and a half years.

It'd been electrifying. Physical, demanding, consuming.

Utterly sublime.

Twelve years ago her kiss had been sweetly innocent with a hint of the spice to come. Now her flavour was piquant, rich and complex.

Terri tasted *right*.

He wanted to kiss her again, explore the spark between them. To rejoice in being alive and savour the stirring of his masculinity.

But they had some issues to sort out first.

Luke huffed out the breath. He was sorry he'd upset

her. The last thing he wanted was to hurt her. He needed to talk with her, find out what the problem was, help her deal with it.

He made up his mind. She had until tomorrow to calm down. Then he was going to apologise for ambushing her and get to the bottom of her reaction.

He walked out slowly to find Mick.

The next day, Luke spotted Terri at the bench in the emergency department kitchenette. He ran his eyes hungrily down then back up the green scrubs that draped her slender body. He smiled wryly. She had no business looking so damned desirable in the baggy work gear. Her hair was caught in a loose bun at the nape of her neck and he itched to tug out the tortoiseshell comb holding it in place, sink his fingers through the long silky strands.

He took a deep breath and dredged up some self-control. He was here to apologise, smooth over any awkwardness. Not create new problems. He needed to talk to her, pave the way for them to discuss what had happened at the race-track.

Arranging his face in what he hoped was an affable, non-threatening expression, he went into the room. Her head was bent, the nape of her neck looked so vulnerable he wanted to reach out, to comfort. She seemed to be staring into the drink she was preparing. She held an empty teaspoon over the rim of her mug as though she was trying to decide what to do with it.

'Terri?'

She started violently, jerking the handle of the mug in her hand. Dark liquid slopped over the bench. She muttered something under her breath, put the teaspoon down and reached for the dishcloth.

'Luke.' A quick flush of red ran under her pale skin.

He stopped beside her. 'I'm sorry,' he said gently. 'I didn't mean to startle you.'

'Did you want something?' Her voice was even as she mopped up the spill. The pattern on the bench would be scoured off if she was any more thorough.

He stifled a sigh. 'I wanted to see you—'

'Well, here I am.' She still hadn't looked at him.

'I wanted to see how you were.'

'I'm fine.'

'Terri…' Voices in the doorway made him glance round. At least one of the people obviously intended to come into the room and Luke didn't want to be interrupted or risk the discussion being overheard. 'We need to talk. Somewhere private.'

'Talk? As hospital director to doctor on duty or something else?' She rinsed the cloth under the tap and hung it over the tap.

Refusal was plain in her stiff spine and he was tempted to lie. 'Something else. Personal.'

'In that case no, I can't spare you any time just now.' She topped up her mug from the urn, then flicked him a brief glance. 'If you'll excuse me…'

He held his hand out in a motion of appeal and she froze. Then took a small step back and looked at him fully. Her eyes were puffy and tired and all the colour had drained out of her cheeks. She looked fragile, as though she hadn't slept well.

He nearly groaned with the need to put his arms around her. 'Terri—'

'I need to go. Please.' The words were calm. Yet he had the distinct impression she was holding herself together by willpower alone. Guilt stabbed at him.

'Of course.' He curled his fingers into his palm and dropped his hand. She waited until he stepped aside before she moved past him.

His gaze followed the graceful sway of her hips until she turned into one of the offices. She must intend to catch up with some paperwork.

He ran a hand through his hair and smiled philosophically.

Terri wasn't going to make it easy for him.

Sue-Ellen would have. His wife had smoothed his life for him wherever she could. He'd appreciated it. Their love had been a quiet, comfortable emotion. Not a grand passion.

Nothing like the volatile mixture of emotions he was starting to feel for Terri.

He sighed. She was complex. Combustion to Sue-Ellen's serenity.

Terri tested the limits of his self-control—which, to his chagrin, were diminishing with each passing day.

What the hell was he going to do about her?

He had to think of something or they were both going to be wrecks by the end of their time together. Though he realised he didn't like thinking of that in terms of a finite period.

CHAPTER EIGHT

TERRI sifted cool sand through her toes beneath a shallow wave. Her walk along the beach had restored a degree of calmness.

Seeing Luke today, being near him after the explosive embrace yesterday, had been impossible. She'd reacted like the gauchest schoolgirl. Embarrassing, but she'd been unable to help it. He'd seen, of course. The pity in his eyes had been hard to take. What did he think of her now? She'd wager that the glowing opinion he'd expressed the other day had been amended.

She turned and walked up to the path through the trees. A small part of her wanted to know what he'd been going to say in the kitchenette. Most of her was just plain afraid. She wasn't sure what scared her the most— that the kiss meant something to him or that it didn't. How contrary.

As she approached the cottage, a figure rose from one of her verandah chairs. She stopped.

Luke.

Her heart stuttered then raced into an erratic uncomfortable riff. Damn, damn, damn. She longed to turn and run, but that was ridiculous…especially as he'd seen her.

Forcing her feet to move, she squared her shoulders and climbed the steps.

'I guess you get to see me after all.' She was proud of the drawl she managed. Her internal tremble was scarcely noticeable. A miracle, considering the way her traitorous heart was still pounding at her larynx.

'I won't stay long,' he said softly, his expression sombre. 'I wanted to make sure you were okay. You were upset today.'

She shrugged, hoping for nonchalance. 'You caught me by surprise after…'

'After yesterday,' he finished for her. 'I owe you an apology for the way I treated you at the track.'

An unexpected dart of pain lanced through her chest. That was one question answered. Her first kiss since her husband's death and the man who'd given it to her was falling over himself to apologise. While he wished it hadn't happened, she'd been shattered by the terrifying beauty and power of it. She couldn't let him see how much.

'Oh, that,' she managed, praying she didn't sound as brittle as she felt. 'Let's consider it forgotten, shall we?'

'I'm not apologising for the kiss, Terri.'

She stared at him, trying to make sense of his words.

'You scared the daylights out of me with the way you were riding that motorbike.' He held up his hand when she would have spoken. 'I know. You're a good rider. Better than good—you're outstanding.'

'Thank you,' she said faintly. 'I guess.'

'Don't thank me. I wasn't watching you and admiring your technically brilliant performance.' He smiled thinly. 'The way you threw that bike into the corners made me angry.'

'Angry?'

'I don't want to lose you.'

She swallowed, looking away uncomfortably.

'*We* don't want to lose you. Allie and me. We've lost too much already. You're her new best friend and confidante. She needs you, I need…I don't want to see her hurt.'

'Of course you don't.' Her heart melted. He was such a good father. 'Neither do I.'

'I know.' There was a small silence then he smiled at her. A slow delicious smile that curled her toes. Her heart skipped a beat and then tripped over itself trying to catch up. She should excuse herself, send him home now he'd said his piece.

'Do…do you want to come in for a drink?' She heard the words leaving her mouth with a sense of astonishment. 'Er, don't feel you have to…I just…I'll understand if you're busy.'

'Nothing pressing,' he said firmly. 'Thanks, I would like a drink.'

'Right.' She stood indecisively for a moment then turned away to open the door. 'Coffee? Or a cool drink? Maybe a beer.'

'A beer would be great.' He followed her inside. Even with her back to him, she felt as though she was aware of every sound and movement he made as he followed her through to the kitchen.

'I've only got light beer.' She opened the fridge. 'Stubbie? Or would you prefer it in a glass?'

'Stubbie will be fine. Thanks.'

She handed him the bottle. His fingers brushed hers and a ripple of sensation ran up her arm. 'It's, um, a nice evening, let's sit on the chairs out the back.'

'Sure.' He held the door open and ushered her out.

As she settled into the wicker chair, she suddenly realised how romantic the setting was with the rapidly dimming pink wash of sunset. The golden glow from the kitchen light behind them did nothing to dispel the illusion of cosy intimacy. The glare of a harsh fluorescent tube would have helped—but to get that, she'd have to get up and walk past the source of her angst to the switch.

Luke twisted the top off his bottle as he subsided into the chair beside her.

'Cheers.' He leaned forward. There was a small musical clink as he lightly tapped his bottle to hers.

'Yes, cheers.' She watched as he lifted the bottle to his mouth, his lips settling on the rim. Looking away hastily, she took a swig from her own bottle. The liquid fizzed in her throat as she searched for something to talk about.

Something other than the thing that suddenly filled her mind.

His mouth, his lips.

His kiss.

Seconds crawled by as she sat in tongue-tied discomfort, her mind utterly stuck on the interlude in the garage. She glanced sideways at him, only to find him watching her intently, his face thoughtful.

She could almost see him gathering words for a discussion she didn't want to have. Not the kiss. She really *didn't* want to discuss that.

'Terri—'

She had to forestall him. 'Do you think you'll ever get back on a motorbike?'

As soon as the words left her lips, she felt ill.

He grimaced. 'I'm not quite ready for that yet.'

'Oh, God. Luke.' Her voice shook with her distress. 'I'm so sorry. I don't know where that came from.'

'Don't worry.' He lifted one shoulder. 'The thought did cross my mind at the track. That was before I saw you, of course. Then all I could think of was talking some sense into you.' He gave her a lopsided smile. 'And look what a good job I did of that.'

She wet her lips. Oh, dear. He was back to the kiss, she knew it. Talking about it meant acknowledging it out loud, holding it up to the light for examination, making it even more compelling. She wanted it to fade away. As it would surely do given enough time and *no* discussion with the man who'd made her feel so raw and conflicted.

When she didn't say anything, he said, 'Refusing to discuss it isn't going to make it go away, Terri.'

She raised her eyebrow and sent him a sidelong look. 'How can you be sure?'

He laughed softly. 'I know some of how you're feeling. It's a shock, isn't it?'

'A shock. Yes, that's one way of putting it,' she said with a sigh of resignation.

'It's two and a half years since I lost Sue-Ellen. I loved my wife. You're the first woman I've kissed since my wife died, and you knocked me sideways. I never expected to feel this way again. Ever.'

Terri contemplated the bottle she held loosely in her hand. Luke and Sue-Ellen had obviously had a very happy, loving relationship. Terri was surprised by the shaft of grief she felt. By the time the landmine explosion had killed Peter, she and her husband had had no marriage left to betray. Her stomach cramped at the memory. She was a fraud, letting Luke assume she was in the same predicament as he was.

He was right about one thing, though. Her equilibrium hadn't been this upset by a kiss since she'd been…

Eighteen, and it had been his kiss then, too. Heat swept through her.

'What I really want to do is kiss you again,' he said. 'Soon. I would do it right now, in a heartbeat, if I thought you would let me. But I'm guessing that's not going to happen…is it?'

'No. Oh.' Her pulse bumped hard. *He wanted to kiss her again.* 'You shouldn't. We mustn't.'

But it was what she wanted too—regardless of all her good sense telling her otherwise.

'I figure I'll give you a bit of time to get used to the idea.'

Her breath caught. 'G-get used to the idea?' she managed.

'Before I do it again.' His eyes tracked down to her mouth and lingered there for a moment.

'I'm only human, Terri, and I'm attracted as hell to you. I've tried to ignore it but that isn't working for me.' He tilted his head, giving her a self-deprecating smile when she remained silent. 'Am I mistaken in thinking you feel the same way?'

'We can't do anything about it. We mustn't.'

'Why not?' He paused. 'Do you feel like you'd be betraying Peter?'

Coldness gripped her at the sound of Luke speaking her late husband's name.

'That's…' Her throat closed and she had to force the words out. 'It's…not the same.' She stood and held out her hand. 'It's getting late. Have you finished your drink?'

He frowned, staring up at her for a long moment before slowly handing over his empty bottle.

She knew she was handling it clumsily but for the life of her couldn't think of a smoother way to signal that the evening was over. She walked past him, into the house. Hopefully, he would go now.

Bottles in hand, she walked to the sink and stopped.

'Not the same...how?' Luke's voice was soft, persuasive.

She turned slowly to see him standing across the room, just inside the door. His expression was tender with sympathy she didn't deserve.

How? Such a simple little question. But the answer had the power to rip her apart. Could she bear to see disgust in his eyes once he knew?

She was a foolish woman who'd stayed too long in a danger zone.

A sad, tragic creature who'd been too slow to accept her husband didn't want her or the baby she carried.

Her folly had cost her everything. Her marriage, her husband.

And the biggest price of all, her baby.

Perhaps Luke had been right that evening in her lounge. Perhaps he did need to know the worst about her. As a colleague, as her boss, as a friend. Maybe most of all as the doctor to whom he'd entrusted his daughter's well-being.

'My marriage wasn't like yours, Luke. We had... problems.' How laughably feeble and mild that sounded.

Solemn blue eyes examined her face calmly. 'Tell me. Whatever it is. I won't think less of you.'

Her throat closed on the urge to be sick. She knew better. Her hands tightened on hard smoothness and she looked down, surprised to see she still held the bottles.

'Peter was taking me to the airport when the explosion happened.' Her larynx felt raw and tender. 'I wanted to come home. He d-died because I wanted to come home.'

'Oh, Terri.'

In two strides, he was there in front of her. She watched numbly as he removed the bottle from one hand then the other. With her hands empty, he gathered her into his arms. His body heat was startling.

'You can't think that way,' he said. 'You'll destroy yourself.'

She wound her hands around his waist. With her ear pressed to his chest, she could hear the steady beat of his heart. After a long silence, she said, 'We were arguing when the car hit a l-landmine.'

'Poor sweetheart,' he murmured. 'And you feel bad because of that.'

She didn't deserve his understanding. She had to make him see, push out the ugly facts until he turned from her as he should. 'If he'd been p-paying more attention, he might have seen something to warn him, a flaw in the road surface. Or something.'

'Hush.' Luke hugged her tighter. 'You know it's pointless to think like that. He probably wouldn't have seen anything. That's why mines are such bloody awful weapons. You know that.'

His body curved over hers, holding her as though she was precious, reminding her of the way he'd been so protective with Allie. With his strong nurturing instinct, he was so unlike Peter.

Peter had loved mankind. He hadn't had time to cater to the needs of a wife. His need to serve had been noble and laudable but so very hard to live with. She'd felt petty and selfish asking for more for herself. For needing more.

Being enveloped in Luke's caring was glorious.

And it was torture.

She wasn't entitled to his good opinion. He still didn't know everything.

She swallowed and gathered the courage to let go the next piece of poison. 'I was leaving him, Luke. My marriage was over. I c-couldn't be the person he needed me to be. I failed him. I f-failed…I failed.' The words to make him understand the rest choked in her throat.

'No, you didn't. Marriages don't always work, sweetheart. It's sad but it's life.'

He thought she'd finished but she hadn't. She couldn't bring herself to tell him the worst. She'd failed again. She was a coward.

His warm hand cupped her neck, the fingers stroking her sensitive skin gently. She stood passively in his arms, her attention on each delicate movement, storing the sensory memories for the future.

'What's so bloody unfair for you is the way you lost Peter and the timing. But it's not your fault, Terri.'

'Don't.' She squeezed her eyes shut as a hot lump in her throat threatened.

'Don't what?'

'Just don't.' She turned her head, pressed her hot face into the cool skin of his neck, feeling the steady bump of his carotid pulse against her forehead.

He shifted and her awareness of the hard body clasping hers changed abruptly. Her pulse sped up.

She should pull back…started to move. His head bent slightly and his breath whispered across her cheek. If she tipped her head a little and reached up, she'd be able to press her mouth to his.

It wouldn't be right to take more than the comfort he'd

given so generously, especially when she had so little to offer in return.

But suddenly she didn't care. She wanted something for herself. A kiss, his kiss. Whatever he was prepared to give her in this moment. She wanted to feel desirable again, to remind herself how that felt.

She tilted her chin, but still he didn't move. Another millimetre nearer and still he waited with infinite patience. Each beat of her pulse pushed her a little closer.

And then the perfect, heart-stopping moment when her lips touched his.

Just the gentlest caress, the barest pressure. Exquisite. His mouth moved on hers, rubbing, nibbling, until the nerve endings in the sensitive skin were alive.

A gift to herself. The beauty of it held her enthralled. She whimpered when he pulled back. Not enough. More. She wanted more.

His hand lifted to tidy a strand of her hair. She suppressed a gasp as he tucked it behind her ear. As his fingers touched the rim, she could feel the tremor in them. Her heart squeezed painfully.

His hand dropped back to her shoulder and after a moment he said, 'I should go.'

'Should you?'

'Oh, God. Terri.' With his forehead resting on hers, he rubbed his hands slowly up and down her arms. 'This is too important for us to rush. I don't want you to do anything that you'll regret.'

'I won't. I wouldn't be.'

He pulled back and looked down at her. His throat moved in audible swallow and then he smiled. 'Don't tempt me,' he said with mock severity. 'I'm trying to do the right thing here.'

'I know.' If she pushed him now, he would give her what she wanted—sweet relief from the thoughts in her head. He was as vulnerable to the chemistry between them as she was. But she couldn't do it, he deserved more.

'We need to talk some more before we go any further.'

'Luke…' She suppressed a sigh. 'You can't solve everything by talking about it.'

He cocked his head, his smile teasing. 'Is this the same woman who solved my problems with my daughter by getting us talking?'

'That was different.'

'In some ways. We do have to talk and we will, but not now.' He pressed a quick kiss to her forehead and stepped away from her. 'Sleep well, darling.'

'Yes,' she said, knowing she wouldn't. 'Thank you.'

'My pleasure.' He reached out again and stroked his fingers down her cheek as if he couldn't resist touching one more time. 'See you tomorrow.'

'Sure. Tomorrow.' Terri watched him go, knowing it was for the best. Much as she ached for his embrace, he was right. She should be grateful he'd decided to leave before she did something they'd both be sorry for.

She wondered what he'd have done if she'd begged him to take her to bed. If she'd begged him to help her forget for a whole night. Not just the precious minutes when his kindness, his touch, his kiss had given her respite from her pain.

She'd wanted to be selfish. To beg, cajole, humiliate herself, until he gave her more. Until he gave her everything.

Her marriage had been far from a meeting of soulmates. Friendship with Luke was richer and more fulfilling than all the sacred vows she'd taken with Peter. Too valuable to risk on the fleeting satisfaction of something more physical.

Besides…Luke was her boss, her colleague. And most importantly, Luke was a father with a daughter who needed him very much right now.

Terri took a deep breath and faced the truth. The last thing Luke needed was someone as broken as she was, clinging and demanding his time and attention.

Luke jammed his hands into his jeans pockets and took a deep lungful of air. The sweet smell of freshly mown grass mingled with the damp of the evening, helping to soothe his frazzled nerves. Leaving Terri was torment. But if he was to have any integrity at all, he had to.

He blew out a long breath.

She'd opened up to him, told him things that made his gut ache with the agony of them. He'd held her slender frame, felt the silent bottled-up grief in her trembling body, and he'd wanted to weep for her. Regardless of the state of her marriage, having Peter ripped from her life like that was a tragedy almost beyond comprehension.

Any hopes, any dreams, any chance of reconciliation had been lost in an instant. Cruel, senseless, irrevocable.

He was almost sure there was more. But why hadn't she told him? She was a very private person. Perhaps telling him as much as she had was all she could handle to start with. He could respect that and when she was ready to tell him more, he'd be there for her.

They'd made a start and he'd been content with that…
Until she'd instigated the kiss.

Then his altruism had evaporated and he'd wanted everything a red-blooded man wanted from a beautiful woman.

He'd wanted to break all his self-imposed rules.

He wasn't proud of himself. Knowing that, given the tiniest bit more encouragement, he'd have taken shameful advantage of a grief-stricken widow.

He'd nearly been unmanned when she'd looked up at him with her big brown eyes. She'd seen worse things than he could imagine. He'd wanted to take away her pain and heartbreak. To hold her, kiss her, touch her.

But he knew it wasn't that simple and, rather than risk the small progress they'd made, he'd chosen caution. It had taken all his strength to let her go, do the honourable thing. He didn't want her to do anything she'd regret. Their relationship was new, complex and far too fragile for a quick tumble into bed.

Why, then, did he have the nagging feeling that he'd let her down tonight?

His restraint hadn't been what she'd wanted, but he knew it was what she needed. Could she have read his retreat as rejection?

His footsteps slowed. He could go back, explain he wanted her more than life itself. Explain he wanted them to get it right, that it was too important for a quick grab at gratification.

Undecided, he stood looking at the cottage then with a small sigh he reluctantly turned for home. Going back now wouldn't be a good idea.

He'd make sure they talk again soon.

He'd make sure she understood how much he wanted her.

CHAPTER NINE

THE next day, Terri hung her white coat on the hook on the clinic-room door and turned to look at her reflection in the mirror. She smoothed her hair, straightened her shirt and ran a quick eye over the profile of her lower half in the new black jeans.

Then she looked herself in the eye and wrinkled her nose. How much more comfortable it was to fuss with her appearance than to think about the thing that was really bothering her.

Luke.

She didn't want to run into him yet. Last night he'd seen her at her worst. She'd been so vulnerable, so needy.

She didn't want to remember that he had the strength to resist her advances. He did a charming line in rejection, very gentle but firm. She grimaced. Too much self-respect to allow himself to be used. She should appreciate that... she *did* appreciate that. But a tiny part of her couldn't help but think it would be nice to have someone lose their head over her...just a little.

At least she'd slept well last night and for that she was grateful to Luke, his insight, his pushing. It had helped rather than harmed to talk about Peter. She'd expected to relive the explosion in vivid, torturous nightmares after Luke had gone. But she hadn't. Her sleep had been dreamless and refreshing.

She moved across to the desk and stacked the patient records she'd used that morning. Scooping them up into her arms, she walked to the door.

With her hand on the knob, she paused and took a deep breath. No point skulking in the office. Seeing Luke was unavoidable as they were both on duty for the day. Her only hope was that he'd been called out for an emergency case but that seemed unlikely as she hadn't been notified that she'd need to take cases from the second list.

She marched out of the room and was nearly at the front desk when surprise had her halting in mid-stride.

'Uncle Mick.' Perhaps she wasn't finished after all. 'What are you doing here?'

'Tee.' His smile was quick and nervous, almost guilty.

'Have you got an appointment now?' she asked. 'I didn't see you on my list but I can see you now if you like.'

'Um, no. Didn't want to trouble you, love. So, I, um, well, you know…should be running along.' Colour ran into his cheeks and he shuffled his feet.

'Are you sure? You seem upset.' Terri was perplexed.

'Fine, I'm fine, love. I just…' Her uncle cleared his throat and then his gaze slid past her. His expression was a mixture of relief and consternation. 'Um, thanks, Luke. I'll, er, catch up with you about those results.' His face turned even redder. 'See you at the track, Tee.'

Frowning, she watched him hurry away. She turned to see Luke slide his used files into the tray. He added a couple of blood tubes to the laboratory test basket. She glanced at the name on the top file.

'Uncle Mick's been to see you?'

'Yes.' Luke looked a little uncomfortable. 'Look, let's grab a cuppa and have a chat.'

'Is there a problem?'

'No, of course not.'

Her spirits plummeted. 'There must be if he's asked to see you. It's just that I thought after I'd diagnosed his diabetes…he's been feeling so much better… Oh, dear, this is such a backward step—I thought he finally believed that I knew what I was doing after all.'

'He does. Your uncle has nothing but praise for you.' Luke leaned across and wrapped his hands around the records she held. She released them quickly as his fingers brushed the skin on her forearm. He placed the files into the tray and said, 'On second thoughts, let's have lunch. We've got some other things to discuss as well and—'

'But he can't be happy with me if he's come to see you.'

'Terri, there are some things that make a man draw a line.'

'Oh. Is he still embarrassed about the incident the other night?' She frowned. 'I thought we'd got past that. I told him it wasn't his fault. That he only behaved that way because he was so ill.'

'Yes, but that's not why he didn't want to come to see you.'

'Then there was another reason?' She suppressed a squeak of surprise when Luke took her by the elbow and ushered her towards the door.

'Nina, we're going for a bite of lunch at home. Page us if you need us.'

'Sure thing, boss.'

'I'm…I don't know if I want to eat lunch with you.' Feet still moving in the direction he was guiding her, Terri looked back over her shoulder at the grinning nurse.

'Sure you do. I make a mean cheese omelette and we've got the kitchen to ourselves today as Mum's taken Dad into Melbourne for a check-up. And besides, you want to know why Mick's been to see me.'

'Yes, I do, but will you please stop making a spectacle of us by dragging me around the hospital?'

He muttered something under his breath and released her. He stopped when she did, a muscle in his jaw rippled giving the impression of tightly leashed emotion. They stood alone on the pavement between the hospital and his parents' house.

'Terri, Mick is fifty five years old.'

'I know.'

'So don't you think that he might be a little uncomfortable getting his first routine prostate check from someone who used to run around in the backyard with his own children?'

'Oh.' She swallowed, feeling like an idiot. She was dimly aware of his hand in the small of her back ushering her down the path. 'Of course. How stupid of me.'

'It's thanks to you that Mick was in here getting the check-up today,' Luke said evenly. 'He said, apart from the hiccup after the races the other night, he's never felt better. *There might be something in this prevention is better than cure rubbish.*' He opened the back door of the house and gently steered her into the kitchen. 'That's a direct quote.'

'Oh.'

'His coming to see me had nothing to do with lack of faith in your ability, Terri.'

A quick expression flitted across her face. If he'd had to define it he'd have said it was pain. Her vulnerability punched him again.

'Well, that's…good, then.'

He saw the faint frown on her face as she stood in the kitchen, looking around. She looked lost, almost as though she wasn't sure how she'd got there. God, he wanted to look after her, protect her, smooth out the bumps in her life for her. He'd set himself a hard task. Terri Mitchell was fiercely independent.

At least, with the surprise of Mick's visit, there hadn't been a chance for her to feel any awkwardness after last night. He'd wondered how their first meeting would go this morning. One bump had been avoided but it had created another that he didn't understand.

'Now, cheese, onion, mushroom?' He turned to the fridge and put the items on the bench as the reeled them off.

'I'm sorry?'

'For the omelette I'm making you for lunch.'

'You don't have to make me lunch.'

'Here's the grater for the cheese. We don't need much,' he said, pleased when her hands automatically began the task he'd set for her. He started breaking eggs into a bowl. 'This is a good opportunity for us to talk.'

'Actually, you're right. We *do* need to talk.' She stopped grating. 'What on earth were you thinking when you told Nina you were taking me home for lunch? She was grinning like the Cheshire cat. Heaven only knows what rumours will have started circulating by the time we get back to work.'

'I don't care.' He wiped the mushroom caps then sliced them thinly with a sharp knife.

'What do you mean, *you don't care*. This isn't London,' she said tartly. 'We're doctors in a small community. You *have* to care.'

'Nope. Do you want to cut up the onion for me?' He looked at her hopefully.

'No, damn it, I don't want to cut up your blasted onion.'

'Pity. Okay, I'll do it.' Suppressing a smile at her palpable frustration, he began slicing the vegetable thinly.

'Luke. Are you listening to me?'

'Absolutely.' He leaned down and got a frying-pan out of the cupboard and put it on the stove over a low heat. 'You're worried that the hospital grapevine has got us over here indulging in a bout of hot sex.'

A quick glance showed him that she was standing with her mouth open. He would be willing to bet that it wasn't because she was speechless. Much more likely that she had too much to say and didn't know which scathing retort to fire at him first.

'Knives and forks in that drawer, salt and pepper on the worktop.' He whisked the eggs and tipped them into the warm pan. Using a spatula, he lifted the edge of the mix to stop it from sticking.

With the eggs cooking gently, he risked another look at Terri. 'Don't you think the people you've worked with for six months have a better opinion of you than that?'

'Maybe.' She sighed. 'Probably.'

He spread the chopped and grated filling over the top of the egg and reached up to grab a couple of plates out of the cupboard. With a deft flip, he folded the omelette then cut it.

'Let's eat,' he said, carrying the laden plates across to set them on the table.

Terri followed slowly and slipped into the chair opposite his. 'Thank you.'

'*Bon appetit.*' He reached for the pepper. Out of the corner of his eye, he could see her pick up her utensils.

They ate in silence for a few moments.

'You're right, you do cook a mean omelette,' she said. 'It's delicious. Thank you.'

'My pleasure.'

Feeding her filled him with a warm glow. Basic, instinctive. Primal. He was surprised how much he wanted to provide food and shelter for this woman. Get close to her, to pet her and love her. To have her return his feelings.

He waited until she took the last mouthful of omelette. There was no easy way to start this discussion so he may as well plunge right in. 'If we're going to have a relationship, we need to set some ground rules up front.'

She stared at him, her mouth stopping briefly in midchew, then he could see her trying to force the food down her throat.

He got up to fill a glass with water then took it back to the table and held it out to her. 'Here.'

She waved it away. 'A relationship? Are you crazy?'

'No, not at all.' He put the glass on the table. 'We agreed last night that we're attracted to each other. There's chemistry between us.'

She gave him a hunted look and pushed away her plate. 'Yes.'

'Good.' He let out his breath. For a moment he'd thought she was going to deny him, but she was no coward.

'Luke, this is a small country town. We work together. You're my boss. Any sort of entanglement outside work has disaster written all over it.'

'We'll go slowly, be sensible. Start off with normal social interaction. Everyday, routine stuff. See where it takes us.' He watched the expressions flit over her face. 'I'm not suggesting that we flaunt it with public displays of extravagant affection but neither do I want to hide it away as though it's a furtive hole-in-the-wall affair.'

'What if we get down the track and realise it isn't working?'

'We're adults, professionals. We deal with it.'

She looked at him sceptically. 'What about Allie?'

'She'd be delighted. My daughter thinks you're the best thing since sliced bread. I know you care about her and I know that wouldn't change.' He leaned his elbows on the table and looked into her eyes. 'Even if you thought her father was the biggest swine this side of the black stump.'

She gave a snort of surprised laughter. 'And is he?'

'He tries hard not to be.'

Terri was still looking at him doubtfully, but Luke sensed he'd crossed some invisible boundary with her.

He smiled. 'So how about it?'

'Slow and sensible?'

'As you want.' And may the powers give him the strength to keep his word without causing him physical injury.

A loud discordant beep made her start. She reached for the paging unit on her waistband and looked at it. Tucking it back into position, she got to her feet. 'I'd better go.'

Hell. Was she going to leave him in limbo? Luke swallowed and stood to pick up the plates. Surely she wouldn't be so cruel.

A second later she looked him squarely in the eye. 'All right, then. Yes. Slow and sensible.'

He stifled the yell that threatened to rip out from gut level and managed a moderate 'Great.'

She nodded. 'See you back at work.'

'Yes.'

As soon as the door closed behind her, he let his smile escape. *Yes!* Now all he had to do was get the balance right. He didn't want her to feel crowded or stampeded by him, but he did want them to spend as much time together as they could.

* * *

Terri's heart somersaulted wildly. She'd just agreed to have a relationship with Luke Daniels. Should she applaud herself for bravery for taking the step or chastise herself for being foolish? Apologise to Luke for leading him on? For not telling him all the reasons why he shouldn't get involved with her?

She was too weak. The love that shone between him and Allie beckoned her closer. Made her want to catch some of the warmth for herself. Was it so wrong of her?

Somehow she would find the courage to tell him what he had a right to know. Soon. Before they got too deep. First she would store precious bright moments in her memory.

She shivered as she walked through the warm spring afternoon. Was she fooling herself?

Everyday routine stuff, he'd said.

She was very much afraid that the *normal, everyday* could be addictive with Luke.

CHAPTER TEN

FIVE days since Terri had agreed to a relationship with him.

Five days of caution and restraint.

Five *whole* days.

Not long in terms of world affairs. Not even a week.

In terms of self-control, it was an aeon.

Luke looked across to where Allie was showing Terri the information tag on another nursery plant. At his daughter's behest, Terri obediently bent to sniff a white bloom. Helpless to resist, he watched the way her red shorts clung to the curve of her buttocks as she leaned forward. A familiar tug of desire caught him low in his gut and he suppressed a groan. Frustration was his constant companion these days.

He'd played it cool all week, not making any overt moves, not giving Terri any excuses to retreat, to change her mind. The first few times he'd joined her for coffee in the staff tea room, he'd felt her wariness. As though she expected him to say something, do something, in front of the other staff. As though she'd known how hard he'd had to tether his need to stake a public claim on her.

By the end of the week she'd almost relaxed and he congratulated himself that his softly, softly approach was working.

Allie flitted to another plant like an overly fussy worker bee. Her face radiated enthusiasm as she turned over the tag, read it, then moved on. He smiled. She'd inherited her mother's love of gardening.

His eyes slid back to the woman who followed a pace behind his daughter. Long dark hair formed a thick gleaming mantle across Terri's shoulders.

Five whole days since he'd kissed her. Since he'd held her in his arms...threaded his fingers deep in her hair.

The sable silk would look glorious spread over his pillow...as her lips moved in a mysterious, womanly smile, inviting his kiss, inviting his touch. Inviting—

'Dad-dy!'

The plaintive cry slapped him out of his fantasy. He focussed to find himself staring straight at Terri. Her soft brown eyes held a quizzical expression. His pulse stopped and then lurched into an erratic bounding rhythm.

Hell. What was she reading from his face?

He swallowed.

'Sorry, miles away.' He walked towards them, forcing his mouth into the best smile he could manage. It felt feeble. 'What did I miss?'

'I want this rose for Mummy's garden.' Allie looked at him anxiously. 'Do you think Mummy would like it, Dad? It's not exactly the same as the one at home but the colour is so pretty.'

He looked from his daughter's wistful face to the plant with its cluster of small coral-pink buds. 'I know your mum would love it because you chose it, sweetheart. It's perfect.'

Allie beamed. 'Cool. Can we get some small plants, too? I talked to Granddad and he said we should. He gave me a list to choose from.'

'Did he? Then if Granddad said so, we'd better get some.' He grinned.

'We need a trolley. They're over there.' Allie pointed then skipped away.

'It's lovely to see her so happy.' Terri's husky voice sent a quiver down his spine.

'Yes.' He watched as his daughter manoeuvred an awkward flat-bottomed trolley back towards them. He tilted his head towards Terri, his eyes following the line of her jaw to her stubborn little chin. 'Have I mentioned how much I appreciate you giving me my daughter back?'

'You might have a time or two.' Her grin was alive with mischief.

'Perhaps I should mention it again,' he murmured, reaching out to capture a ringlet of hair that had caught on the simple gold chain of her necklace. Masculine satisfaction surged at her quick shiver as he stroked the strand back over her shoulder.

'It's not necessary.' There was a slight catch in her voice and when her eyes darted up to his they held a dark flare of awareness.

His gaze moved down to her mouth, watched as she caught her bottom lip. Her teeth sank into the tender flesh until he wanted to protest, wanted it to be his teeth nipping at the plump cushion.

'Terri—'

She blinked and looked away, a strained smile curving her mouth. 'Well done, Allie. Let's grab your rose and see what else we can find.'

Rooted to the spot, Luke watched as one of the attendants lifted the pot of the chosen rose onto the trolley. His daughter chattered to Terri and pushed the trolley a little further along the aisle. When they stopped, a trick of the light bathed the two of them in a glowing, ethereal halo. Terri bent her head towards Allie, whose upturned face was filled with trust and hope.

And love.

He stared at their smiling profiles. The seconds moved with a syrupy slowness as his heart compressed painfully. A shudder ran through him as though a foundation had shifted deep in his psyche.

He blinked and looked away, waiting for normality.

He wanted Terri badly.

He ached for her, but this sensation was something more. Something powerful, elemental.

Frighteningly important.

He'd promised to take things slowly and sensibly but there was nothing temperate about the emotions storming through him.

He frowned, abruptly certain he didn't know enough about her. She'd opened up so much the other night. Wrenching details about her marriage and about her last moments with her husband. Was there more? If there was, she'd baulked at the idea of sharing it with him. Why? What could be worse than the things she had told him?

Perhaps his unease was because he sensed the trauma of the explosion and her husband's death had left Terri with even deeper emotional scars than those she'd revealed. How could it not? Did a soul ever truly heal from such cruel wounds?

Despite the heat of the sun on his back, a chill spread across his skin. As though an unseen threat lurked just beyond his comprehension.

He huffed out a long breath, shrugging away the shiver of unwelcome intuition. The only thing he could do was take it one step at a time, build trust, hope they'd create something worthwhile together.

'Okay, you two, let's get this show on the road.' He aimed a smile at them as he strode forward. 'Plants. We need plants. Allie, you've got the list so you're in charge of choosing. Terri, you're with me behind the trolley.'

Allie giggled and relinquished the handle to him.

Luke captured Terri's hand and tugged her to his side. 'Now I've got you right where I want you,' he said under his breath so only she could hear.

'Luke!' Her gaze flew to where Allie was comparing a tag to the list she held.

'What? I'm only holding your hand.' He gave her a wicked grin. He lowered his voice and said, 'Would you like me to show you what I really want to do?'

'No,' she all but yelped. 'No, absolutely not. Behave.'

'Then you'd better hold my hand tight, hadn't you, sweetheart?' he said, his gaze roving over her anxious face.

'What about Allie?' Terri's eyes were fixed on his daughter. She cared very much for Allie's well-being.

Suddenly his peculiar mood dissolved and he relented. 'Don't worry. I've had a talk to her about going out with you.'

'You have?' Terri's eyes came back to his, wide and uncertain.

'She thinks it's a good idea. In fact, I think I've gone up in her estimation. See what a good influence you're being on me.'

'Mmm.' Her lips pursed in a moue of doubt and his pulse spiked. *Conversation, concentrate on the conversation.*

'Yes, she even wanted to give me some dating advice.' He strolled down the aisle towards Allie, who had moved on further. 'I should take you to the movies and buy you ice cream apparently. It's what all the girls like.' He gave Terri a thoughtful glance. 'What do you think...will it get me to first base?'

'Not likely,' she muttered darkly. 'You promised we wouldn't flaunt it.'

'I also said we wouldn't hide it.'

'I think we need to have a discussion on definitions. Yours versus mine.' Her tone was astringent. 'I'm starting to sense a lack of compatibility.'

'I'm always ready to discuss our relationship with you.' He grinned at her. 'Just say the word.'

He laughed when his impertinence was rewarded by an old-fashioned look. This subtle dance of courtship between them was a pleasure. It had been a long time since he'd done something just for the fun of it.

At the checkout, he said casually, 'Mum's issued a not-to-be-refused invitation to you for dinner tonight. Hasn't she, Allie?'

'Oh, yes, please come. Ple-ease,' said Allie.

'Dad said you used to be a regular at *chez* Daniels before we arrived.' It was short notice and his pressure was less than subtle, but he didn't care. He didn't think Terri was the type to play games. If she was free, she would come. If she wasn't, he wouldn't like it but he'd have to be philosophical. He layered on some more pathos. 'We'd hate to think we'd scared you off. Wouldn't we, Allie?'

'Yes.' His daughter looked faintly confused but game to agree.

'Since you asked *so* nicely, I'd love to,' Terri said, her narrow-eyed stare letting him know exactly what she thought of his tactics.

He grinned, unrepentant, and tried hard not to look

too smug. Judging from the look Terri gave him, he hadn't succeeded.

He was falling hard and quick. Too hard? Too quick?

His senses told him Terri Mitchell was solid gold. His doubts weren't about her. They were about her past and the pain she was still carrying.

With care and patience, they could handle anything that was thrown at them. He was sure of it...

He pushed away a second shadowy whisper of pre-science.

CHAPTER ELEVEN

'TERRI! You're here!' squealed Allie.

Luke's head snapped around as his daughter dropped the cutlery she'd been setting out on the table to race over and hug their guest. Hard to believe from Allie's behaviour that she'd seen Terri only a matter of hours ago. Though he certainly couldn't chip her on her over-enthusiasm, given the great line of somersaults his own gut was doing.

'Come and see where we've put the rose I picked for Mum,' said Allie. 'We planted it as soon as we got home. Granddad had the garden all ready.'

'Give Terri a chance to say hello to everyone else before you start dragging her off, Allie,' Luke said, placing the chairs he'd been carrying around the table. *Give her a chance to say hello to me.*

'Hi, Luke.' Terri's smile was wary as he drew near and put his hand on her shoulder. He leaned forward to give her a peck on the cheek. Low down, right beside her mouth. Her skin was soft beneath his lips. She smelled delicious, fresh soap, light fragrance. All woman. All Terri.

'I brought a bottle of wine.' She stepped back and thrust a bottle into his hands.

He looked at the label, giving himself a precious moment to regroup. A South Australian white wine. 'Thanks. You must be psychic. Mum's baking fish on the barbecue.'

'Not so psychic.' She grinned. 'I spoke to Vivienne when we got home from the nursery earlier.'

'Clever, then.'

The back door opened. 'About time you showed yourself around here, young lady,' said Will as he carried the large bowl of salad to the table and then crossed to hug Terri. 'I was starting to wonder what that new hospital director had done with you.'

Unexpected heat crept into Luke's face. He knew what the new director had been doing with her.

And what he planned to do, given half a chance.

'Oh, just the, um, usual. You know, work, work, work,' Terri said with a weak laugh. Her cheekbones flushed becomingly as her eyes slid in Luke's direction and then quickly away.

Will frowned. 'Humph. I still say the board did the wrong thing by you.' Luke stifled a sigh when his father shot him an ambiguous look. 'I told Luke he was stepping on toes. You did an excellent job as acting director.'

'Thank you, Will, but it's working out well having Luke in charge.' This time, when she slanted a look at Luke, she met his eyes. He enjoyed the tiny conspiratorial moment. 'We've got the new boy licked into shape now and you know how much I detest paperwork. We don't let Luke go home until he's cleared his desk.'

'Like me with my homework,' said Allie with a big grin. The way his father and daughter responded to Terri was beautiful.

'Exactly like that.' Terri smiled as she ran a hand down Allie's stubby ponytail. 'Yes, I think your father's proving to be quite satisfactory, Allie.' She looked at him from under her lashes. 'All things considered.'

'Thank you for that faint praise,' Luke murmured, feeling close to tongue-tied. She was flirting with him. His heart wobbled and then melted.

'Oh, it's important to give encouragement…where it's deserved, of course,' she said, obviously struggling to keep a straight face. Her lovely brown eyes were alight with laughter. 'And a reprimand where it's not. I'm sure, as the new director, you'd agree, Luke.'

'I do agree.' Luke smiled, sending a promise of private retribution in his gaze.

Her answering smirk had his overworked pulse leaping about in anticipation.

His father's expression eased into a relieved grin. 'As long as the two of you are working it out.'

Luke could see Terri's teasing had been a thousand times more effective than all his attempts to soothe his father's concerns.

'Now, can I show Terri the garden?' said Allie in long-suffering tones.

'Sure,' said Luke. 'Don't be too long, though. Dinner's nearly ready.'

'Come on, Terri.' Allie took Terri's hand and tugged her along the path.

As they disappeared round the side of the house, his father said, 'Perhaps I should go, too. Terri might appreciate my tips for growing roses.'

'Perhaps another time, Dad.' With only the smallest trace of guilt Luke handed the wine bottle to his father. 'Terri brought this. Would you mind putting it on ice?'

He set off down the path after Terri and Allie, leaving his father to draw his own conclusions.

* * *

'Oh, this is gorgeous,' said Terri, when she saw the neatly laid-out garden.

'Dad put up the arch and we both planted the rose. See, it'll grow up all over the trellis.' Allie waved her hands expansively to demonstrate. 'I put in the little plants where Granddad said. And we have this bench. Come and try it.' Allie sat on the concrete seat and patted the area beside her. 'There's thyme on the ground underneath. It grows flat so when you stand on it, it smells nice.'

'You've all done a fabulous job.' The fresh clean aroma of the herb rose to greet Terri as she sat on the bench.

'Yes.' Allie's face held deep satisfaction. 'Dad said Mummy would like it.'

'I'm sure he's right,' Terri said, a lump in her throat. Sue-Ellen had been a much-loved wife and mother. What a wonderful epitaph to have earned.

'Yes.' Allie leaned sideways and rested her head on Terri's upper arm.

The simplicity of the moment was a gift that had Terri's heart stuttering. A snug, warm band tightened around her chest as she looked down on the dark head.

'And how are *you* now, Allie?' she asked softly.

'I'm good. Daddy said you and him might go out sometimes.'

'Did he?' Terri swallowed. 'Well, we might. Is that okay with you?'

'I think it'd be cool and I'd be able to come, too, sometimes, wouldn't I? Like today with the plants.'

'Of course. I'd like that.'

Terri looked up and saw Luke. He'd propped one shoulder against the smooth trunk of a gum, hands in the pockets of his jeans. He'd obviously showered and changed not long before she'd arrived because his hair was still dark and spiky with dampness.

His face, as he looked at Allie, glowed with love and pride. But when he moved his eyes to her, Terri read something different altogether. Dangerous. Seductive. Irresistible.

Her heart jolted, her defences crumbling. In that moment she realised she had little hope of protecting herself against this man and his daughter. By sharing themselves so unconditionally, they'd made a serious chink in her armour.

It was more than she'd ever thought she'd have in her life.

More than she deserved.

A shadow passed over her spirits. Would she end up letting them down, failing them in some way she couldn't predict?

She would have to make sure she didn't.

Terri worked her magic effortlessly on his whole family, Luke realised as he looked around the table a couple of hours later.

He took a sip of wine as he watched his mother. Her face was alight with laughter at something Terri had said as the two of them stacked the dishes from the meal.

His mother obviously adored Terri…and this from the woman who'd given him and Kevin such a hard time about their motorcycles.

Carrying a pile of plates, Terri set off towards the house. Luke ran his fingers absent-mindedly over the rounded belly of his wineglass and down the stem to the base as his eyes followed her slender figure. She moved gracefully with effortless elegance. Womanly curves, nicely proportioned. Long, long legs. He suppressed the urge to gulp. Altogether a *very* nice package.

'Earth to Luke?' He started slightly and glanced up to find his sister standing beside him, a grin on her face. 'Have you finished with your glass?'

He handed it over silently and Megan walked after his mother and Terri.

His sister. Another member of his family under Terri's spell. It was Megan who had sensed that Terri might help Allie. By taking her down to visit at the beach cottage, a link had been established between his daughter and the woman who had saved her life only a matter of days later. That link had set up the trust that had enabled Allie to confide her agonising guilt and set her on the road to recovery.

His father had thawed completely after Terri's banter. Anxiety that she felt displaced by the hospital board's decision was understandable. At least now, with concern eased, Luke would be able to get a better idea of how the man was coping psychologically after the heart attack. It was a relief because the faint ongoing hostility hadn't been good for any of them.

They were all putty in Terri's hands—including himself. Any way she wanted to handle him was just fine with him. Any way at all. The sooner the better for his sanity…

'Nice girl.' His father broke into his thoughts. 'Something special.'

Luke swallowed and hoped the rush of heat warming his face wasn't visible in the dusk. He yanked his thoughts back into line and looked across at the older man.

'Terri,' his father clarified, arching one eyebrow at him.

Luke cleared his throat. 'Yes, she is.'

'Allie likes her.'

'She does.'

'So does your mother.'

'Mmm.' Luke looked into his father's interested gaze. 'What are you getting at, Dad?'

'Nothing. Just making an observation.' Will brushed the leg of his shorts. 'Your mother would like to do some travelling.'

'Would she?' It was a curious segue. Luke wondered what was coming next.

'She's been at me again to retire.'

'Has she? How do you feel about that?'

'I used to think it was a ridiculous idea.' He sighed then continued after a moment, 'But since the heart attack…'

'You're thinking about it seriously, then?'

'Today, anyway.' A wry smile curled his father's mouth. 'Maybe tomorrow I'll change my mind. Anyway, I thought I'd float the idea at you, just in case. I'm sure the board would look favourably on you taking the director's job permanently. If you wanted it.'

'Okay. Thanks for the heads up.'

'Would you want it?'

'I'm not sure, Dad. I'd have to think about it. Sound Allie out. I promised her we'd only be here for a year.'

'She seems to have settled in.'

'She has now.' *Thanks to Terri.*

There was a companionable silence for a few minutes and then his father said, 'Well, it's something for you to think about.'

'Yes, it is.'

The back door opened and Terri came out with a coffee pot in hand. Allie, her faithful shadow, was beside her, holding the sugar bowl. His mother followed a few steps behind with the mugs.

Conversation meandered through various topics for another half an hour and then Terri stood.

'I should make tracks,' she said, turning to his mother. 'Thank you for a wonderful evening, Vivienne.'

'You know you are always welcome, Terri. Don't be a stranger.'

Luke rose, too. 'I'll walk you home.'

'Oh, no need.' Terri tucked a curl behind her ear. 'I can practically see my place from here.'

'That's a good idea, Luke,' said his mother. Luke blessed her and her fondness for observing the niceties. Never mind that Terri wandered backwards and forwards between the hospital and the cottage at all hours of the night when she was on call.

Good manners would be observed. And in this case, it definitely worked to his advantage.

He smiled at Terri, who made a small grimace at him.

'I'll be back shortly, Allie,' he said.

'No worries, Dad.' Allie beamed at him. 'Don't hurry. I'll go up to bed.' She gave a theatrical yawn. 'You can kiss me goodnight when you come back.'

'Er, right.' He stared at her as she kissed her grandparents.

Confident of her welcome, Allie walked over and put her arms around Terri's waist for a quick hug. 'Thanks for coming shopping with us today.'

'Thank you for asking me, Allie. I enjoyed it.' Terri smiled, her face soft with affection as she looked at his daughter.

'Goodnight.' With one last fierce look at him, Allie set off towards the house.

As he crossed the grounds with Terri, Luke was aware of everything about her. The way her slim arms swung slightly at her sides, the way her hair slipped forward when she bent her head.

'This is so silly, you walking me home.' Her voice was light and quick.

He detected the tiniest tell-tale catch. Wicked anticipation curled through his gut. 'It's what a well-mannered boy does at the end of a date.'

She rolled her eyes at him. 'This wasn't a date. It was an invitation from your mother, I seem to recall.'

'Ah, good point. That makes it even more significant than any ordinary date.' He nodded sagely. Out of the corner of his eye, he saw her misstep and reached out to steady her.

'Sorry?'

'You've had your feet under my parents' dining table.' He left his fingers curled around her arm as he expanded on his theory. 'In dating traditions, that's an important milestone.'

There was a small silence and then she teased, 'Does it count when it's outdoor furniture? Surely it's much too casual.'

'A table is a table. Tradition isn't fussy.'

'It certainly isn't when you're making up the rules.' She laughed as they approached the narrow line of trees that separated the house from the lower yard.

'Tsk. I'm starting to wonder if you're going to renege on that other time-honoured end-of-date tradition.' Her cottage was just ahead. Too close.

'It depends *which* tradition you're thinking of,' she said, not backing down an inch. '*Some* traditions might earn you a slap for your trouble.'

Heat sizzled along his nerve endings as his imagination conjured a scenario that would definitely earn him a slap. He swallowed the groan that crept up his throat. Being with her like this made him want to throw caution to the winds and find out.

'That's not what you said the other night.' He followed her up the front steps.

'That was then. This is now. Besides, a gentleman wouldn't remind a lady of her moment of weakness.' At the door, she turned to face him.

He braced his hand on the frame and looked down at her. Her light fragrance teased his senses. He resisted the urge to lean forward and breathe deeper. 'I'm not feeling much like a gentleman tonight.'

'Aren't you?'

'Nope. Invite me in.'

'And find out? I don't think so.' She flicked her hair back in a quick nervous gesture that made his pulse leap. 'You're in a peculiar mood.'

'Yeah, I am,' he murmured, reaching out to run his fingers along her jaw. 'So how are my chances for a kiss goodnight, then?'

'If we're taking things slow and sensible, they should be zero.' Her voice was ragged as he curved his fingers around the back of her neck and tilted her chin up with his thumb.

'Should be?' He bent and brushed his mouth across hers. Once, twice. She resisted him. On the third brush, her mouth softened, moved. Heaven. Sensitive nerve endings in his lips revelled in the warmth and sweetness. His muscles quivered as he ruthlessly suppressed the need to take more, take it deeper.

Take it all.

He caught her lower lip between his and sucked gently before moving his mouth across her cheek to the column of her throat just below her ear. When she arched her neck slightly to give him better access, he nibbled his way down to the nape.

'Oh. You are too good at this,' she moaned as a shudder ran through her. 'W-we should s-stop now. Please.'

He took a deep breath, inhaling her scent as he reached for control. He closed his eyes and rested his forehead in the curve of her shoulder. Her skin felt warm and alive beneath his brow.

'This is a bad idea.'

'Right this minute, it feels pretty good to me.'

'Yes,' she breathed. 'Me, too.'

He pressed his lips to her throat, felt the frenzied beat of her carotid pulse, felt her muscles move in a swallow. His heart leapt with the confirmation that she was as affected as he was.

'But that's in *this* moment.' Her voice was more determined. She shifted, inching away.

He let her. She was going to make him go. He moved back, his hand still braced on the doorjamb. His eyes moved over her face, taking in each fine feature. 'You don't think we should seize the moment, explore the possibilities.'

'It's not necessarily a bad thing. To leave possibilities unexplored.'

'Only if we're faint-hearted. Are we going to be faint-hearted, Terri?'

'Tonight? I…Yes. Yes, I believe we are. Goodnight, Luke.' She groped behind her back and the door swung open. He saw a gleam of white as she smiled then backed inside. 'Thank you for the escort home. See you on Monday.'

He smiled back. 'Monday.'

The door closed gently. He lifted his hand, spread his

fingers on the wood and after a moment said softly, 'Lock your door, Terri.'

'I will.' Her voice came from just the other side of the door.

The latch clicked into place. In spite of his frustration there was some small comfort in the thought that she'd loitered there. Was she as torn as he was? He'd like to think so.

Terri pressed her hand to her sternum, feeling her wild thump of her heartbeat begin to settle as she listened to Luke's footsteps.

She felt so much, wanted so much when she was near him.

He made her wonder just how truly deep and beautiful a relationship between a man and a woman could be. Made her wonder what it could be like between *them*.

How foolish she'd been to think they could agree on slow and sensible and keep things under control. Her hunger was unnerving and she sensed Luke's matched it. They were both too eager to take the next step.

It had taken all her willpower to resist inviting him inside.

Regardless of how tempting it was to throw caution to the winds, there was too much at stake for both of them. Professionally, personally and emotionally.

CHAPTER TWELVE

Two weeks later, Luke shrugged into his grey suit jacket and straightened his red tie.

Red for confidence, red for determination.

Red for passion and daring.

Excitement spiralled through his lower abdomen. He hadn't been this wound up about a date since he'd been a teenager.

An evening with Terri. Alone. Just the two of them… He chuckled softly. And a restaurant full of people, of course.

He picked up his car keys and wallet from the end of the bed then walked along the hall to his daughter's bedroom.

'Allie, let's go.' He tapped at her door. There was no reply. 'Allie?'

The door was slightly ajar so he pushed it open to see his daughter sitting on the edge of her bed, looking glum.

He frowned. 'Honey, what's wrong?'

'Nothing.' She studied the tips of her new sandals, refusing to meet his eyes.

She'd been fine half an hour ago when he'd gone to have his shower and get dressed for tonight. What had happened between then and now?

'Are you sick?'

A shake of her head.

He crossed to sit beside her, his hand automatically moving to her forehead. Her skin was cool to his touch and she wasn't having any obvious trouble with her breathing.

Silent alarm bells went off. Was it a return to the troubled days where Allie had been sullen and uncommunicative? His earlier excitement fizzled out abruptly. He wasn't going to leave it this time. He wasn't going to let her shut him out.

Maybe Allie didn't like the idea of him dating Terri after all. They'd discussed it but perhaps she'd changed her mind now that it was about to happen.

'Come on, Allie. What's going on?'

Her bottom lip wobbled.

'I'm staying right here until you tell me.'

'You can't.'

He took a slow deep breath in and let it out as he strove for patience. He couldn't believe it. Over the last couple of weeks he and Allie and Terri had spent a lot of time together. It'd been fantastic. But now it looked as though Allie's morose mood *was* to do with Terri.

'I can. You and I are getting to the bottom of this even if it means I have to cancel tonight. Terri will understand.'

'Oh, no!' Allie's gaze flew to his, wide with dismay. 'You can't do that.'

Her vehemence made him raise his eyebrows. 'So talk to me.'

She looked back at her shoes. He clenched his jaw and set himself to wait for as long as it took. After a moment, she mumbled, 'I don't see why I can't come, too. I'll be good and I can help.'

'Help?' He heard the strangled note in his voice.

The relief was so overwhelming, he had to work to

suppress a great shout of laughter. Allie was happy for him to go out with Terri—she just objected to being left behind.

'Yes.' She looked at him, her face suddenly alight with enthusiasm. 'You know. With ideas and stuff. We had heaps of fun at the movies, didn't we? And Terri likes me.'

'We did have fun and I appreciate that you want to suggest things to do,' he said carefully. 'But I'd like some time with Terri so we can talk about things that would be boring for you.'

'You mean like work things and that.'

'Like that.' He nodded.

'Will Terri want to do that, too?' Allie looked doubtful

'Yes,' he said firmly. 'She will.'

'Oh. All right, then, I guess.' She plucked the hem of her shorts. 'Will you kiss her?'

Definitely.

Absolutely.

One hundred percent guaranteed.

But was Allie ready to hear that yet? She was used to seeing him and Terri holding hands but was more going to be difficult for her to handle yet?

A split second later, she said, 'I think you should. Otherwise she won't know that you like her.'

He swallowed. 'Okay, then I'll make sure that I do. Are you ready to go over to Nana and Granddad's?'

'Yep.' A small resigned sigh escaped as she stood and picked up her backpack.

'Got your pyjamas? Toothbrush?' He reeled off the items as they walked through to his parents' wing.

'Yes, Dad.'

'Inhalers? Drawing book?'

'Yes, Dad,' she said with a roll of her eyes.

'Pencils, Rubbers? A kiss goodnight for your father?'

She giggled. 'Probably.'

After he'd dropped Allie off with his mother, Luke jogged down the steps to his car.

It was his birthday.

He knew what he'd like from Terri as a present. Perhaps she'd let him put his order in.

He grinned. Or perhaps not.

Whatever happened, he was looking forward to having a great time. Slow and sensible might be agonising for him on one level but it was worth it. Terri was letting down her defences, relaxing with him. That was worth every bit of physical suffering.

Terri's heart lurched when she heard the knock at her door.

Luke.

Fortifying herself with a deep breath, she smoothed her hands down the heavy silk of her cheongsam and walked through the hall.

She'd shared wonderful family outings with Luke and Allie recently but this was different. This was their first real date.

The man waiting for her at the front door was starting to mean more to her than was sensible.

She turned the handle and opened the door, her pulse tripping crazily. He looked formal and so handsome dressed in a charcoal-grey suit.

'Hi.' Her grin felt wobbly.

'Hi, yourself.' His voice was husky. The broad smile on his face faltered as he ran his gaze down her length and slowly back up. 'You look fabulous.'

His eyes were dark and intense when they focussed on hers again, his mouth moving in a small enigmatic smile that had her catching her breath.

'Thank you,' she managed. 'You, too.'

He stared at her a moment longer. 'Ready to go?'

'Yes. I just need to get my purse from the kitchen.' She should have brought it with her to the door, she thought as he followed her down the hall.

She grabbed it off the table and turned to find him right in front her. Her eyes were level with his mouth.

He leaned forward, still not touching her. Her fingers tightened on her purse. The tiny beads pressing into her skin as her breath caught in her chest.

All she had to do was step back.

She didn't move.

His head tilted, moved closer, lips hovering over hers.

Closing her eyes, she waited. Sensations bombarded her, the musky scent of his aftershave, his breath feathering across her cheek.

And finally the delicious touch of his mouth on hers. Light and sweet and lingering with a hint of leashed passion. Her system quaked as she recognised a deep feminine desire to surrender.

He pulled back and she opened her eyes slowly.

'Mmm…nice.' His blue eyes were slumberous and inviting. 'I have it on good authority that's how I can let you know I like you.'

Laughter gurgled up her throat, catching her unawares, relieving the heavy sensual tension. 'Allie's been giving you dating advice again?'

'She has.' He grinned. 'Miss ten-going-on-twenty.'

His hooded gaze slid down to her lips. 'Though I think she's onto something with this idea. I should tell you…I like you.' He waited a beat before adding, 'A lot.'

She laughed again as he waggled his eyebrows at her. 'I'll consider myself duly warned.'

'I was afraid you'd say that.' He smiled wryly and held out his elbow. 'Shall we go? Your chariot awaits, my lady.'

She braced her jelly-filled knees and took his arm, feeling the strength there, allowing herself to be swept along by his old-fashioned chivalry.

Terri followed the waiter through to their secluded table by the large window. Luke's hand was spread over her spine, just below the small of her back. The contact felt intimate, made her acutely aware of her body, her movements. The sway of her hips, the tiny brush of her stocking-clad thighs against each other, the way her buttocks moved with each step she took in her high heels. Did he realise how astonishingly seductive it felt? She wanted to wiggle, just a little, to see if he would slide his hand even lower.

Heat raced across her skin, radiating out from his hand and spreading deep into her abdomen. She took a quick gulp of air and huffed it out. She didn't have to worry about Luke behaving tonight—she was doing a fine job of seducing herself.

Regret and relief vied for the upper hand when the wicked, tempting hand was removed so Luke could pull out her chair.

'Thank you,' she murmured. She looked around as Luke took his seat. The restaurant was in an old converted warehouse adjacent to the wharf. The seafaring theme was tastefully done with gleaming brass fixtures and dark wood panels. Strategically placed fishing nets had been draped across the upper walls with glass floats dotted here and there.

Candles in thick glass bowls graced each table and cast a romantic light.

'I'd heard this place had been done up,' she said, meeting Luke's gaze across the table. 'I've been meaning to come here for a meal.'

'I brought Sue-Ellen—' He stopped, his mouth twisting in a grimace. 'Sorry, I didn't mean…It's not a good way to impress my date for the evening, is it?'

'Don't apologise. Why wouldn't you mention her? She was a big part of your life. Yours and Allie's. It's good for Allie that you talk about her mother.'

'Thank you.' His voice was gravelly. 'You're a very special woman, Terri.'

She grinned, making light of the comment. 'I'm glad you think so.'

The waiter returned with the menus and wine list.

'Any preferences for wine?' Luke asked.

'White as we're having seafood but other than that I'm leaving it entirely up to you.' She looked over the delicious selection of dishes on her menu.

The waiter took their orders and returned a few minutes later with the bottle of wine. He filled their glasses and snuggled the bottle into the ice bucket. When the man had gone, Luke lifted his glass.

'To us. To slow and sensible.'

To slow and not so sensible. Terri bit her tongue to prevent the amended toast from escaping. She quickly tapped her glass to Luke's and concentrated on the wine. The cool rich liquid left a delicious lingering taste of oak. 'Mmm, lovely. Good choice.'

She met his eyes across the table. 'Allie's spending tonight with Vivienne and Will?'

All night?

No, no, no. She *wasn't* going to ask that. She didn't need to know.

'Reluctantly, yes.' Luke gave her a wry smile. 'She

wanted to come with us to make sure we had fun. She's worried about whether I'll be able manage on my own.'

'Ah, more dating advice?'

'Yes. We…' He cleared his throat and she wondered what he'd been going to say. After a moment, he continued, 'I must remember to remind her about this in a few years when she starts dating.'

Terri chuckled. 'She'll be mortified.'

'I'm counting on it.' His quick laugh made her pulse skip.

He put down his glass and reached across the table to cover her hand with his. His voice was soft and husky as he asked, 'So, how am I doing? Are you having fun?'

'Oh, definitely.' With an effort she managed to keep her tone light. 'I promise to send you home with a glowing report card, lots of gold stars.'

His eyes sparkled with a dark, sensual invitation. 'In that case, I promise to do my best to earn every single one.'

Her heart did a slow, painful somersault into her throat, completely blocking her ability to reply.

When his hand slid away from hers a moment later in a smooth caress, she nearly protested. It wasn't until his gaze released hers that she realised the waiter was standing beside them, holding their meals.

She let out a slow breath and looked at her wineglass. Only one tiny sip and good sense had deserted her. She felt sinfully frivolous, intoxicated. *Luke*. She was tipsy with the heady influence of his company.

'Thank you,' she murmured to the waiter as she smoothed the napkin on her knee. She'd ordered pan-fried fillets and they looked delicious with their crispy, golden-brown coating and side order of thick roasted-potato wedges. A bowl of tossed salad sat in the middle of the table for them to share.

'Everything all right?'

She looked up to see Luke watching her. Her world seemed to tilt even further off its axis.

'Yes, perfect.' She forced her mouth into what she hoped was a reassuring smile and picked up her knife and fork. 'This looks wonderful.'

Now all she had to do was eat it. Laughing and flirting with Luke had wiped out her appetite for food completely.

'Did I tell you Dad's talking about retiring?' he said.

Thank goodness. A *safe* topic. Something to take her fertile mind off her overwhelming sensual awareness of the man opposite her.

'Is he?' She cut off a small forkful of fish, relieved when it melted in her mouth and slid easily down her throat.

'Mmm.'

'I know your mum would like him to take things a bit easier but I got the impression that he was adamant that it wasn't going to happen any time soon.' A second mouthful. She was getting the hang of this.

'He's mentioned it twice now with no prompting so I think he's seriously considering it.'

'Viv would be pleased, even if he only scaled back his hours.'

'Yes, she would.' Luke rested his knife and fork on the edge of his plate and reached for his wineglass.

There was a small silence during which Terri managed another couple of mouthfuls.

'Dad asked if I'd be interested in staying on in the director's position.'

The potato seemed to congeal into an unswallowable lump in her throat.

Luke.

Staying here.

Not going home to England. She couldn't make up her mind if it was excitement or dread fizzing along her nerve endings.

She grabbed her glass and took a mouthful, using it to push the potato down her throat. 'Did he?' She put her glass back on the table. 'What do you think you'll do?'

He shrugged slightly. 'I'm not sure. There's no hurry to decide right now, but it's something to think about.' His gaze captured hers. 'It's been good to come home.'

Her chest tightened. She looked down at her plate, went through the motions of taking another forkful of food. 'How do you think Allie would feel about it?'

'I'd have to talk to her, of course.' He swirled the liquid left in his glass. 'But again, it's not something I need to do immediately. She's made great progress since you got us talking. I don't want to throw anything disruptive into the mix yet.'

'Yes. Although I think she's quite resilient now that burden of guilt has gone. She's really blossoming.'

'She is, isn't she? Maybe I'll sound her out to see if her ideas about Port Cavill are more open now.' His smile was filled with affection. 'What about you?'

'Me?' Her eyes flew to his. 'You have to make the best decision for you and Allie.'

'That's true.' His eyes narrowed and she had the feeling his attention was suddenly scalpel sharp. 'But what I was really asking was, what is your vision for *your* future?'

'Oh.' She pushed half a wedge of potato aside then carefully laid her knife and fork together in the space she'd created. Her fingers returned to adjust the position of the utensils before she moved the plate. 'When I came here, I—I didn't have a vision beyond putting myself back together after…'

'After Peter's death?'

'Yes.' She touched the base of her glass, twisting it slightly with her fingertips. 'After Peter's death.'

'What about now?'

'Now?'

'Now that things have changed.' With his elbows on the table, he steepled his fingers and looked at her intently. 'Now that you're in a relationship. How do Allie and I factor in your life?'

'Oh. I'm—I'm not sure I want to look too far ahead.' If she did, she'd have to face the fact that she hadn't been scrupulously open with him. She'd have to face the things she'd baulked at telling him.

His expression fell for the tiniest instant before he covered his reaction. She'd disappointed him, hurt him. Shame cramped deep in her chest. She looked through the window at the lights reflected on the glass-smooth water of the sheltered port. In a way, Luke had offered her a safe place in the haven of his family and all she could do was selfishly protect herself. He deserved better. She wanted to give him something...

'Luke...you and Allie are the most beautiful things that have happened in my life for the longest time.' Her voice choked with emotion. 'You're both very dear to me. More than I can say.'

'Thank you,' he said softly, his fingers curling around hers. His smile was so sweet that the tears gathering at the back of her eyes pressed for release. 'I'm glad. You're very dear to me, to us.'

There was a small silence. Part of her wanted to hide from the power of her feelings. The other part revelled that she could feel so intensely.

'Excuse me, sir, would you like to order dessert now?'

'No, thank you,' Luke said, still not taking his eyes off her. 'I think what we'd like to do now is have a dance.'

'Yes,' she whispered. 'That would be lovely.'

As the waiter cleared their plates away, Luke took her hand and threaded his way through the tables to the dance floor.

Dreamy notes from the string quartet had lured many other dancers to the floor already. He stopped at the edge of the floor and took Terri's other hand, guiding her into his arms. She came to him smoothly, fitted perfectly, as he'd known she would. Her lithe body swayed to the rhythm in easy, seductive movements.

He held her right hand, cradling it close to his chest. With his right hand splayed across her back, he felt the deep inhalation expanding her rib cage, then her exhalation whispered on the skin above his collar. A groan lodged in his throat. It was heaven and hell to hold her like this. He smiled slightly. He was going to enjoy every torturous, delicious moment of it.

He tucked her closer. 'This is nice.'

'Yes, it is.'

He could feel her fingers stroke along his collar. God, did she know what she was doing to him? He held his needs on a tight leash. They were making progress. Sure, it was slow but they were working towards something special, something lasting. A grab for quick gratification would ruin that.

He felt another inhalation, a tiny shiver through her slender frame.

'Luke?'

'Mmm?'

Her footsteps slowed to a halt and she leaned back in his arms. Wide and dark eyes looked into his.

'I—I want to stop being sensible.'

A hot streak of electricity jolted through him and his hand tightened on hers. He couldn't have spoken to save himself.

'Take me home, Luke. Please.'

'Hold that thought.' He steered her back to their table where the waiter met them with the dessert menu. 'I'm sorry but we're going to have to go. Would you mind organising the bill for me, please? I'll pay at the front register.'

'Of course, sir.'

Luke helped Terri with her lightweight shawl, his hands lingering on her shoulders before he tucked her hand into the crook of his arm. He was almost afraid to stop touching her in case the loss of contact gave her time to reconsider.

Foolish. If she changed her mind, he would find a way for that to be okay.

He brought her hand up to his mouth, kissed the delicate knuckles then let her go so he could sign the bill.

In the car, he drove feeling the weight of her silence. Was she even now thinking she'd made a mistake? He'd hurried her out of the restaurant with indecent haste.

He glanced across at her when he stopped to give-way to traffic at a roundabout. She was watching him, a small smile playing around her lips. She looked unexpectedly serene while he felt like a bundle of nervous energy.

At the beach cottage, she unlocked the door. He followed her inside, waited while she gracefully slid her shawl from her shoulders and draped it over a hook on the hall-stand.

She turned to face him then stepped close, her hands reaching for his tie.

He laid his hands over hers, stilling the fingers loosening the knot.

'Are you sure?' His voice was husky. How strange, he'd been so worried she'd change her mind but now it was him giving her the opportunity to reconsider.

She sighed, her hands flattening on his ribs. 'Yes. And no.'

'No?' He made an effort to disguise the need that was thick in his voice. Was it possible to die of self-control? 'I don't want you to do anything you don't want to, darling.'

'I want to make love with you, Luke, but I'm afraid I'll disappoint you. I couldn't bear it.'

'You won't. You couldn't.' He gathered her into his arms, feeling his own nerves subside as he searched for the words to reassure her. 'This is us, Terri. Not a competition, not a race. We'll take it slow, we might have some hiccups, but it doesn't matter. We'll get there in the end, darling. Together.'

'Together. I—I'd like that.' Her lips pressed softly to his jaw, sending a thrill dancing through his body. 'Thank you.'

He turned his head, captured her mouth, felt the last tiny moment of hesitation evaporate as her lips opened for him and she kissed him back. She reached up to wind her arms around his neck, her body pressed to his, her breasts flattened on his chest, her belly aligned with his. They stood hip to hip and his heart nearly burst with huge, solid beats.

She pulled away and reached for his hand. 'Come with me.'

He followed willingly and found himself standing in her bedroom. Moonlight shone through net curtains, spilling across the double bed.

'I heard it's your birthday.'

'Yes,' he murmured.

'I—I wondered if you like the wrapping on your present.' She took his hand and laid it on the line of toggles along her collarbone.

'I love it.' He swallowed. 'Am I allowed to unwrap it now?'

'Yes, please.'

His eyes on hers, he released the first fastener. Moved to the second.

Terri ran her hands up the smooth thin fabric of his shirt, feeling the heat of his body on her palms. She released the buttons, impatient now to feel his skin on hers.

This man made her feel so special, so cherished. At this moment she wanted him more than she'd have ever believed possible. She wanted it all. Something to remember, something to hold dear in the future. He treated her with such care and affection that she wanted to weep.

They seemed to fit as though made for each other. No fumbling, no clumsiness. She revelled in his touch, her skin coming alive beneath his clever hands. It was special, satisfying, overwhelming. Enriching. She felt exotic and wicked and daring and courageous. He gave her all of that and more.

Much later, Luke propped himself up on one elbow and looked down at her.

'My head's spinning,' he said, as he leaned forward to kiss her lips.

She looped her arms around his back and smiled, not caring if her heart was in her eyes. 'Mine, too.'

He spread her hair over the pillow, slowly, as though he was enjoying running his fingers through the strands. 'I've been having fantasies about doing this.'

'Really?'

'Oh, yeah.' He smiled broadly. 'Remember that day at the nursery? Allie had to yell to get my attention.'

She laughed softly. 'She did have to call you a couple of times. You looked so guilty when you finally answered.'

His smile slowly faded. 'You know it's too soon for me to spend all night here with you.'

'I know.'

'I'd like to.'

'You've got a daughter who needs to be your first priority and that's the way it should be.'

'As long as you know I want to stay. Maybe, soon—'

'Hush, let's not try to make any time lines, Luke.' She put her fingers to his lips to stop the words. It was too soon and she wanted to revel in this moment. Bask in what they'd created here, together in the cocoon of her room, her bed. She didn't want to think about the outside world, the things she still needed to tell him. 'Let's enjoy what we have. Right now.'

He growled deep in his throat and gathered her close. 'I don't have to leave quite yet.'

'Mmm. Good.' She ran her hands up his back, loving the feel of his hard muscles tensing as he moved over her.

Later, she rolled on her side as he slipped out of bed. With her hand splayed over the sheet still warm from his body, she watched him dress.

'I'm not going because I want to,' he repeated as he shrugged into his shirt. 'Promise me you're not going to read anything into me leaving you like this, darling.'

'I promise,' she said obediently.

He fastened his trousers. 'Why do I get the feeling you're just saying that?'

She laughed at him. 'Now who's reading too much into things?'

'As long as I'm the only one,' he said with a sigh. 'I'll give you a ring tomorrow. We'll do something, a barbecue.'

'Okay.'

'Okay.' He stood juggling his keys in one hand, obviously still reluctant to go. 'Well...goodnight.'

'Goodnight, Luke.'

At the door, he turned. 'Promise me—'

'I do. Now, go home, darling.' She laughed.

'You called me darling.' He came back to the bed and leaned over to press another lingering kiss to her mouth. 'God, I wish I didn't have to go.'

'But you do. Now shoo.'

He sighed. 'Okay. I'll lock the door after me.'

After he'd gone, she flopped back on the pillow and stretched luxuriously. Luke was amazing, he made her feel like the most beautiful woman alive.

She laughed out loud at the happiness that fizzed along her veins.

Love. She was in love. How could she not love the man who made her feel so whole and normal?

A tiny doubt tried to creep in but she refused to let it, refused to listen to the malevolent voice that wanted to remind her about the things she hadn't told him about herself.

She'd faced so much in the last few years...surely she wasn't so bad for wanting to clasp *this* moment for herself, to hold tight to the present, not worry about the past and the future. Just for now.

CHAPTER THIRTEEN

'NO REST for the wicked, you two.'

Terri looked around to see Dianne grinning at them from the doorway of the staff lounge.

'What's up?' Luke said.

'Three victims of a minor MVA on the way in. Details are sketchy but nothing serious by the sound of it. They've been scooped up by a Good Samaritan. ETA about five minutes.'

'Thanks, Dianne.' Luke picked up his mug and took a quick swallow as he rose to his feet. 'I'm on my way.'

'No worries.' The nurse gave them a quick indulgent smile and disappeared.

Terri's heart squeezed as Luke winked at her. He leaned down, his breath whispering over her ear as he murmured, 'I wonder how she knows we've been wicked, darling.'

She inhaled sharply then sputtered when her mouthful of coffee went down the wrong way. As she coughed, Luke helpfully patted her a couple of times between the shoulder blades.

'It might have something to do with being seen all over Port Cavill for the last two weeks holding hands,' she gasped between small coughs.

'Good point. Still, nice to have something true circulating on a hospital grapevine for a change.'

He looked so pleased with himself that she couldn't help laughing. Her own insouciance surprised her. The magic of her relationship with Luke had infected her with a carefree spirit that she hadn't felt for years.

Her gaze followed him to the sink, enjoying a quick feast on the lean length of him. She loved the way he moved, confident and full of masculine grace.

He turned, catching her eye, and his smile filled with mischievous intimacy. 'Relax and finish your coffee.'

'Thanks.' Her cheeks flooded with warmth as she grinned. 'I won't be long.'

A tiny shadow marred her happiness as she watched him leave the room. She still hadn't told him everything. Surely it wasn't so bad if she left it a little longer. Everyday was bringing her a greater sense of belonging, an easiness which meant the words, the courage would come soon.

She sighed as she got up and crossed to the sink. The little pact she was making with herself had disaster written all over it. This weekend. She would talk to Luke this weekend. That gave her just over three days to find the right way to broach the subject.

As she walked down the corridor, she saw Luke and Dianne heading towards the front door. The MVA victims must have arrived. She picked up her pace.

She turned into the main emergency foyer and the scene in front of her exploded into her senses.

A woman. Pregnant. Her groin and legs covered in red. Screams tore at Terri's ears.

'My baby. I don't want to lose my baby. Please, help me. I've hurt my baby.'

The air around Terri's legs turned to heavy syrup, dragging at her steps until she stopped. She felt disembodied. Time jerked past frame by frame.

'Pete! Where's Pete?' the woman sobbed. 'Our baby…'

Images flashed onto Terri's retinas, blotting out the scene before her.

Baby in peril.

Mother injured.

Blood everywhere.

Nausea swept up from her toes. She couldn't do this. Not again. She couldn't help them. She couldn't move.

Each pore on her skin iced over. She was failing.

Again.

Failing.

Luke flicked a glance at Terri.

Something was terribly, terribly wrong. She was rigid, face as white as a sheet, eyes fixed on the screaming woman.

'Terri!'

Oh, God. His voice wasn't reaching her.

He wanted to go to her, hold her, shield her from whatever nightmare was holding her in its thrall. He sensed Terri's crisis was the bigger emergency, but the patient in front of him was rapidly descending into hysteria.

'I've hurt my baby. Please, save my baby.' The woman clutched at his arm, dragging his attention back to her.

'We've got you now,' he said calmly. 'What's your name?'

'N-Nadia.'

'Nadia, we're looking after you and your baby. Are you in any pain?'

'N-no.' She hiccuped and looked at him in surprise. 'Not now.'

As he and Dianne settled Nadia on a gurney, Luke glanced across the foyer. Terri was gone.

* * *

It was paint, for God's sake. Nadia and her husband, Pete, had been travelling with an open can of paint—the pregnant woman had been holding it between her knees so she could stir it.

A contraction had caught them by surprise and Peter had driven into their front fence. With the impact, red paint had gone everywhere. A neighbour had piled the hapless pair into his car and brought them into hospital.

The contractions hadn't continued so no pattern has been established. Luke suspected it had been a set of Braxton-Hicks' contractions perhaps exacerbated by Nadia's fear. They'd keep her in hospital for a few hours and monitor her to make sure everything was as it should be. The baby's heartbeat was strong and regular.

He'd packed Nadia and her husband off to the showers to wash away the last of the paint and now he had to attend to the real emergency.

Terri.

'Anyone seen Terri?'

'I haven't seen her since…the call about Nadia and Pete,' Dianne answered, and the others looked around blankly.

'If you do, page me, stat. Please.' He ground his teeth. 'Same goes for any emergencies. I'm going to find her.'

Aware of the circle of concerned faces, he walked out of the department, leaving no words to soothe their fears. He had none.

Urgency drove his steps. He had to find Terri. She'd been shattered. Something about that case had pushed her into some private hell. He'd seen a glimpse of her terror before she'd disappeared. More than terror, she'd looked in danger of disintegrating.

He worked methodically, checking every room. Would

she have gone all the way home? For some reason he didn't think she'd have been able to get that far.

She'd been like a wounded animal, looking for somewhere to tend her injuries, a private place.

He finally found her outside, behind the new gazebo. She was on her knees with her arms wrapped around her body. He could see her knuckles were white as though by gripping tightly she might hold herself together. But even that self-hug wasn't enough comfort for her. She rocked in a small rhythmic movement that broke his heart.

Weak sun shone on the chocolate of her hair, picking out bright threads of red and chestnut in the thick mane.

He crouched beside her, touched her lightly on the shoulder.

She jerked, her reflex beyond a normal fright response. He could feel the fine tremors that raced through her chilled flesh.

'Terri.'

The rocking started again.

'Talk to me, darling. Please.'

'No p-point. There's no point. It won't help. You can't help me. No-one can. G-go away. Please. Just…go away.'

He sat on the ground beside her, not caring about grass stains, and gathered her rigid body close.

'Tell me anyway,' he said as he rubbed her back.

For the longest silence, he just held her, rocked with her. Hoped that his body heat would help to thaw her.

'S-so much blood.'

'It was red paint.' But she didn't hear him.

'So much blood,' she whispered. 'She killed her husband, sh-she killed her baby.'

'No! No she didn't. Terri, listen to me. Her husband is fine. She's fine. She mightn't even be in labour.'

'But the blood…' She shuddered

He took her face between his hands.

'Terri. Look at me.' Her eyes slowly focussed on him. 'It wasn't blood.'

'N-not blood?' She sounded confused, as though he was speaking a foreign language.

'Paint. It was paint.'

'P-paint?' She tested the word as though trying to divine its meaning.

'Red paint. Nadia was in the car with an open can of red paint between her knees. She was stirring it.'

'I s-saw all the r-red.'

'I know, darling. I want you to come back now.'

'I c-can't. I mustn't. The b-baby…sh-she'll lose the b-baby. You can't trust m-me.'

'What do you mean?'

'B-bad things happen. I killed my husband. I killed Peter.'

'The terrorists killed Peter.'

'And my b-baby. I killed my baby.'

'You lost your baby in the explosion?' Oh, God. How had she coped with that, alone, having just lost a husband as well? His heart ached for her. No wonder she was struggling.

'Yes. My fault. It was all my fault.'

'Why?' He needed to hear it all as much as she needed to tell him.

'I stayed too long. I stayed too long. I should have left as soon as I found out. But I didn't. I killed my baby.'

'Oh, darling, no. No, you didn't,' he said gently. 'You're a wonderful, brave woman who's carried a terrible burden all by herself.'

'My baby. My poor baby.' She made a strangled sound

deep in her chest and then the tears started in huge shuddering sobs. His heart broke for her. Just listening to her story was painful beyond belief. He felt powerless in the face of her grief.

Her arms clung to him, desperation in their strength. All he could do was hold her, be her rock. He was going to stand by her, to help her heal. Hold her when she needed to cry, encourage her when she was moving forward.

He would love her and protect her and support her until she was better.

And then, by God, she was going to marry him so he could love and cherish her as she deserved for the rest of her life.

Her sobs gradually quieted until the only sound was the distant shushing of the waves.

Reluctantly, he broke the moment. 'Do you trust me, Terri?'

'Yes.' Her voice sounded raw from the weeping, still full of tears ready to be shed.

He was going to ask her to do more, to be braver. To do something that he sensed she needed to do. A first minute step on the journey back to normality.

'I want you to come with me now. Come and see the young couple who came in earlier. Nadia and Pete.'

'Nadia and P-Pete?'

'Yes.'

'I can't,' she said. With the storm of weeping over she'd moved into a passive acceptance of hopelessness. 'There's no point. It's over.'

'You can.' He felt like such a bastard asking anything of her when she was so raw and vulnerable. Setting his jaw, he continued, 'Nothing is over. There's every point to coming back.'

It was important not to let her withdraw. He was afraid for her, afraid for himself that he would lose her, if he let her retreat now.

'Come on. Wash your face, powder your nose, whatever it is that you need to do to face the world again today. Just for a few minutes.'

'I can't d-do anything for them. I ran away.' She looked at him through a welling veil of tears. 'I f-failed.'

He steeled himself against weakening. 'You ran away because you're traumatised. You haven't failed. I don't want you to do anything for them, I just want you to come and meet them. Not for long, just to see that they are okay. Come on, Terri. You can do it.'

She looked at him and then finally, she took a deep breath and said, 'I'll try.'

The bravery in those tiny, barely audible words brought a painful lump to his throat. 'That's all I'm asking, darling.'

Anxiety pinched at him as he helped her to her feet. She felt so shaky and frail. The last of her strength and vitality had leached away with her tears, leaving this frighteningly fragile husk.

He clenched his teeth. He needed to find out as much as he could about post-traumatic stress disorder. Stat.

Cuddling her close to his body, he walked her back to the building. Outside the women's bathroom he stopped and opened the door, ushering her inside. 'I'll wait outside. Yell if you need me.'

She nodded.

'I'll check on you in five if you're not out.'

She gave him a wan smile. 'I'll be out.'

'Okay.'

He shut the door behind him and braced one hand on

the wall. Terri needed his help and she was going to get it. Whether she wanted it or not. He was in awe of the fact that she'd come this far carrying the weight of her grief alone. But she didn't have to do it on her own from now on. She had him to help. He wasn't going to let her go. She would not shut him out, he wouldn't let her.

He felt a touch on his arm and turned to see Dianne looking up at him, her face creased with worry. 'Is Terri all right?'

'She's had a shock, Dianne. She'll be shaky for a while but she'll be all right. I'll make sure of it,' he said grimly.

'Good. If there's anything any of us can do, just say the word.'

'Thanks, Dianne.'

Luke kept the visit to the now-sheepish young couple short and upbeat before ushering Terri out of their room.

In the privacy of the staff lounge, he ran the backs of his fingers over her pale cheek. 'Go home, darling.'

'Luke, I think…' She took a deep breath in. 'I think I'd rather keep busy. Please?'

'Terri…love…you've had a hell of a shock. Cut yourself some slack and take the rest of the shift off. It's only an hour.'

She gave him a haunted look.

He stifled a sigh. 'Tell me honestly, do you feel up to being here?'

Her mouth opened then slowly closed, her shoulders slumping. 'No,' she whispered. 'No. You're right. There's no point being here.'

'Darling, go home. Rest, walk along the beach.'

She nodded.

'I'll come and see you as soon as I can.'

Another nod before she turned and walked away. He watched her go. Had he done the right thing? But what else could he do?

She looked so crushed and utterly defeated that he almost called her back.

Just over an hour later, Luke took some correspondence back to his office. A single piece of paper lay in the middle of his desk. Cold inevitability gripped him as he leaned across and picked it up.

A resignation. Neatly typed. Terri must have gone straight home to write the damned letter.

No way was he going to let her run away like this. He couldn't. She needed help and support from people who loved her. Specifically, she needed *his* help, *his* support. He loved her.

He practised the persuasive words he'd use as he walked down to the beach cottage. When he got there the door was ajar but the place had an oddly deserted feel.

He knocked. Icy fear thrummed through him when there was no response. He yanked open the door then strode from room to room.

No sign of Terri but plenty of signs that she'd been here and been busy.

A suitcase lay open on the bed they'd made love in. Folded clothes sat in piles, waiting to be added to the case. As though she'd started packing but had been distracted from the task.

In the kitchen, pots and pans had been thrown haphazardly into a box on the bench. There was no chance that the lid could be fastened with the way handles bristled above the sides. At the other end of the bench was a stack of plates and a collection of glasses.

Without pausing, he opened the back door and stepped on to the verandah. A half-empty mug of coffee sat on the edge. He could imagine her sitting here drinking it, staring towards the beach. Was that where she was now?

His pulse fluttered as he jogged off the verandah towards the trees. He didn't know what to expect, refused to think about what he might find.

She would be there.

She *would* be there...

And she was.

The tension in his body loosened abruptly, leaving his gut aching and his knees rubbery. She was sitting on the sand, hunched over with her arms wrapped around her shins as she stared out to sea.

Jamming his hands into his pockets, he took a deep shuddering breath. Damp, briny sea air filled his lungs and he stood for a moment collecting his wits before he walked closer to his still oblivious target. When he was several feet from her, he stopped. Keeping his tone carefully neutral, he said, 'You've been busy since I saw you.'

She started as though he'd yelled at her.

'You know I'm not going to accept your resignation.' He stepped forward and lowered himself to the sand beside her, but not touching.

'You should.' She sounded so cold, so remote.

He had to connect with her so that she would listen to him.

'Why should I?'

Her head came around at his question and she looked at him. A frown slowly pleated her forehead as she thought about her answer. 'Because I can't be trusted. My judgement is flawed.' She shrugged and turned to face the water again. Her voice was too matter-of-fact for the agony behind the words she spoke. 'I'm so brittle I feel like I could fly apart.'

'Terri, you're suffering from post-traumatic stress disorder.'

She didn't acknowledge him.

He tried again. 'You need to get help so you can recover.'

Her gaze stayed on the horizon.

'You have so much courage. I'm asking you to use some now.' He watched her profile for any sign that he'd reached her. 'For me and for Allie. We need you. *I* need you.'

'Allie.' She shook her head and her chin trembled for a tiny fraction of a second. 'I don't know if I can be whatever it is that you need, whatever it is that she needs. You can't trust me to make good decisions.'

'I *can* trust you. I *do* trust you. It's you who doesn't trust you. And you should. You have wonderful judgement. Your thinking is just a bit scrambled at the moment because of your experiences.'

'You make it sound easy.' She shook her head. 'But it's not. I'm empty. You and Allie deserve more than I can give you.'

'Not true, darling. We deserve you. You're the person who saw what my daughter and I needed. You're the person who brought us together after months of grief.' He felt as though he was fighting a battle with no weapons, nothing to hold onto, nothing to let him see if he was making headway. He was losing her. 'I know it's not easy. I hear your pain, I felt your heartbreak when you cried in my arms.'

'Stop. Luke—'

'I know I can't understand what you're going through.

But I know this, I'm here for you' He swallowed, feeling the crushing pain in his chest. 'I love you, Terri.'

Her hands came up to cover her face and her shoulders began to shake. *He'd reached her* but in doing so he'd given her more pain.

He pulled her into his arms and laid his cheek on her hair as he absorbed the tremors that shook her.

'It's okay, darling, it's okay.' He murmured the words over and over, knowing how very far from the truth they were.

At last, her sobs quietened.

'I feel broken.' Her voice was still thick with tears.

'You're in pain, darling, but the bits of you are all there. We'll find help and you can put them all back together again.'

'I feel so bad.' She took a deep shaky breath. 'What if I can't be fixed? What if this is me? What if…I can't be a doctor any more?'

'Then you can be anything you like.' He stroked her hair. 'Be my wife.'

He felt shock ripple through her. He hadn't meant to say the words, not yet. But it was what he wanted. After a moment, she tipped her head back and looked at him.

'Marry me,' he said.

'Oh, Luke.' Her face screwed up in pain. 'I w-want to accept your proposal s-so badly. But I c-can't. It wouldn't be fair.'

Pain squeezed his chest. 'To whom?' he asked softly.

'To you, to Allie.' She looked into the distance. 'Maybe even to me.'

'Can you tell me why not?' He smothered the fear that clawed at him and held onto one tiny skerrick of hope. She hadn't refused him outright.

'Because I don't think I know who I am any more. I

need help to find out.' Her eyes came back to his holding a plea for understanding. 'What if I've changed? I'm not sure I can handle the weight of your disappointment.'

His spirits swooped but he made himself give her a nod of reassurance. 'Then let's find you some help and see where it takes you. I want to marry you, Terri. The offer is there, no expiry or use-by date. And no pressure.'

'Thank you.' Her face was sombre.

He tightened his arms around her in a quick hug. 'In the meantime, I have more news,' he said dragging up the first change of subject that occurred to him. 'Ah, make that I have *lots of news* since I haven't told you what led up to it. Allie and I have been talking about staying in Port Cavill. We'll be house-hunting at the weekend. We want you to come.'

'You're staying? And you've talked to Allie about it?'

'Yes and yes. Um, I've been meaning to tell you,' he teased gently. 'But when I'm with you, I get sidetracked with other things.'

'Luke, that's wonderful.'

'I thought so.' He grinned at her. 'So how about it? Will you come with us? You'll know about workable room layouts and Allie tells me you have better decorating ideas than I do—you know, colours and that sort of thing.' He dragged out his best hopeless male look.

'I—I think I could manage that.' A relieved smile lifted the exhausted lines on her face.

His heart swelled with love. More than anything, he wished he could take away her sorrow and self-doubt. All he could do was wait, be there for support and encouragement.

And hope that when it was all over, he had a place in her life, her future.

Her heart.

CHAPTER FOURTEEN

Two months later.

'NOT there, Dad.'

Luke looked up from the bucketful of damp sand he'd just deposited at the intersecting corners of castle wall. 'What's wrong with here? I like it here.'

Allie giggled—a lovely warm happy sound. 'It's all wrong. It needs to be back further. We'll ask Terri.' She looked around to see if her consultant was back yet. 'She'll know how it should be.'

Luke suppressed a smile. Allie was right, Terri would know.

She'd been involved in every step of the house-hunting and under her inspired guidance the house had been decorated to suit a family. A perfect home for his family. Himself, his daughter…

All it needed was a wife. And the perfect candidate for the post was coming through the tree line at the top of the beach, carrying a picnic basket.

'Okay, time for a break, workers,' Terri called. 'Come on. I've got sandwiches, watermelon, fruit juice and biscuits and fresh coffee.'

'Now you're talking.' He loped over to shake out the mat they'd brought down earlier. As soon as he'd laid it Terri and Allie lowered themselves into neat cross-legged positions. He sat beside Terri, his arm resting on his raised knee.

'Dad's put the corner thing in the wrong place, Terri.' Allie accepted a thick salad sandwich.

'Has he?' She looked at him under her lashes. 'Tsk. It's hard to get reliable serfs these days. So perhaps you can have two walls. You'll just have to get your dad to cart more sand.'

'Cool. That's what we can do, Dad.'

'Mmm, why didn't *I* think of that?' He sent a smouldering look Terri's way as she passed the plate of food to him.

She grinned and helped herself to a sandwich. 'Well, if you'd put the turret where you should have in the first place…'

He tugged the hair in the centre of his forehead. 'I'll try to do better, mistress.'

'Glad to hear it.' She exchanged a laughing look with him and his heart turned over. She was beautiful.

He was very proud of her. He wondered if he realised how far she'd come in the past two months. A spiral of excitement corkscrewed through him.

Day by day, she was relaxing a little more, gaining resilience, losing the haunted, frail look.

At the hospital, she was doing marvellous things. They'd discussed her hours and he'd pressed for her to come off the shift roster. But she'd been more than pulling her weight with running health clinics, reaching out to disadvantaged members of the community, organising preventative health initiatives.

In his life… He hadn't been pushing for intimacy in their relationship, knowing that he had to leave the pace up to Terri. Last night they'd made love. A thrilling heat ran through him at the memory of pleasure beyond anything he'd known. If he spent the rest of his life worshipping her with his body he would be a very happy man.

After lunch, he cradled his coffee mug and watched Allie at the sandcastle. She had been joined by another couple of children and the three of them were working diligently.

'She's doing well,' Terri said.

'Very.' He swallowed the last of his drink and put the mug aside. 'Those breath exercises you taught her have been terrific. She's chasing me to make sure she does them.'

'Good for her. She's been one of my best pupils.' Terri laughed self-deprecatingly. 'But, then, I might be a little biased.'

The words gave him a warm glow. Terri cared, wanted the best for Allie and for him.

God, he loved her so much. He…

'Marry me.' He heard the words leaving his mouth, saw the twist of anguish flash across Terri's face.

In that one spontaneous moment he'd ruined everything. Why couldn't he have waited? Too late, he wished he could call the words back. He felt sick. She was going to say no.

'Luke…' She stopped, closing her eyes, gathering herself.

He should help her, say it was all right, say it didn't matter…that they'd still be friends.

But he couldn't do it—not even to spare the woman he loved from the agony of having to refuse him. His face felt numb as he waited for the sentence that would rip his heart out.

'You've been wonderful and I wouldn't have got this far so quickly without your support.' Her throat worked and he could see she was struggling to say the words. 'There's something that I have to tell you, something I've been hiding…even from myself.'

She looked at him and the sadness shadowing her eyes clawed at his gut. 'When I lost my baby…the placenta was ripped from the wall of the uterus… Luke, I don't know if I'll be able to have children.'

A family with him.

She wanted to have a family.

With him.

She looked at him solemnly. 'I can't marry you unless you know that. I don't want it to come between us down the track.'

'I don't care.' He caught her by the upper arms and pulled her into his embrace. 'I don't care. It's you I want. Only you. If we had children together that would be wonderful, too. But it's you I want.'

With his face buried in the crook of her neck and his eyes squeezed shut, he took a deep breath. 'I'll sorry if it turns out that you can't have children, but for you, darling, not for me. You'd be a wonderful mother.'

He pulled back and looked at her. 'I love you. Marry me.'

Her eyes sparkled with unshed tears. 'Yes. I love you and I'd love to marry you.'

'Yes!' He leapt to his feet, tugging her then scooping her up to twirl her around.

'What are you guys doing?'

'Allie.' He laughed then sobered. He'd started preparing his daughter for this possibility but had he done enough? 'Allie, sweetheart, we're going to get married.'

'It's about time,' she said and her face split in a huge smile. 'I suppose this means you're too busy to come and carry sand.'

APRIL 2010 HARDBACK TITLES

ROMANCE

The Italian Duke's Virgin Mistress	Penny Jordan
The Billionaire's Housekeeper Mistress	Emma Darcy
Brooding Billionaire, Impoverished Princess	Robyn Donald
The Greek Tycoon's Achilles Heel	Lucy Gordon
Ruthless Russian, Lost Innocence	Chantelle Shaw
Tamed: The Barbarian King	Jennie Lucas
Master of the Desert	Susan Stephens
Italian Marriage: In Name Only	Kathryn Ross
One-Night Pregnancy	Lindsay Armstrong
Her Secret, His Love-Child	Tina Duncan
Accidentally the Sheikh's Wife	Barbara McMahon
Marrying the Scarred Sheikh	Barbara McMahon
Tough to Tame	Diana Palmer
Her Lone Cowboy	Donna Alward
Millionaire Dad's SOS	Ally Blake
One Small Miracle	Melissa James
Emergency Doctor and Cinderella	Melanie Milburne
City Surgeon, Small Town Miracle	Marion Lennox

HISTORICAL

Practical Widow to Passionate Mistress	Louise Allen
Major Westhaven's Unwilling Ward	Emily Bascom
Her Banished Lord	Carol Townend

MEDICAL™

The Nurse's Brooding Boss	Laura Iding
Bachelor Dad, Girl Next Door	Sharon Archer
A Baby for the Flying Doctor	Lucy Clark
Nurse, Nanny...Bride!	Alison Roberts

0310 Gen Std LP

MILLS & BOON

APRIL 2010 LARGE PRINT TITLES

ROMANCE

The Billionaire's Bride of Innocence	Miranda Lee
Dante: Claiming His Secret Love-Child	Sandra Marton
The Sheikh's Impatient Virgin	Kim Lawrence
His Forbidden Passion	Anne Mather
And the Bride Wore Red	Lucy Gordon
Her Desert Dream	Liz Fielding
Their Christmas Family Miracle	Caroline Anderson
Snowbound Bride-to-Be	Cara Colter

HISTORICAL

Compromised Miss	Anne O'Brien
The Wayward Governess	Joanna Fulford
Runaway Lady, Conquering Lord	Carol Townend

MEDICAL™

Italian Doctor, Dream Proposal	Margaret McDonagh
Wanted: A Father for her Twins	Emily Forbes
Bride on the Children's Ward	Lucy Clark
Marriage Reunited: Baby on the Way	Sharon Archer
The Rebel of Penhally Bay	Caroline Anderson
Marrying the Playboy Doctor	Laura Iding

0410 Gen Std HB

ROMANCE

Virgin on Her Wedding Night	Lynne Graham
Blackwolf's Redemption	Sandra Marton
The Shy Bride	Lucy Monroe
Penniless and Purchased	Julia James
Powerful Boss, Prim Miss Jones	Cathy Williams
Forbidden: The Sheikh's Virgin	Trish Morey
Secretary by Day, Mistress by Night	Maggie Cox
Greek Tycoon, Wayward Wife	Sabrina Philips
The French Aristocrat's Baby	Christina Hollis
Majesty, Mistress...Missing Heir	Caitlin Crews
Beauty and the Reclusive Prince	Raye Morgan
Executive: Expecting Tiny Twins	Barbara Hannay
A Wedding at Leopard Tree Lodge	Liz Fielding
Three Times A Bridesmaid...	Nicola Marsh
The No. 1 Sheriff in Texas	Patricia Thayer
The Cattleman, The Baby and Me	Michelle Douglas
The Surgeon's Miracle	Caroline Anderson
Dr Di Angelo's Baby Bombshell	Janice Lynn

HISTORICAL

The Earl's Runaway Bride	Sarah Mallory
The Wayward Debutante	Sarah Elliott
The Laird's Captive Wife	Joanna Fulford

MEDICAL™

Newborn Needs a Dad	Dianne Drake
His Motherless Little Twins	Dianne Drake
Wedding Bells for the Village Nurse	Abigail Gordon
Her Long-Lost Husband	Josie Metcalfe

MILLS & BOON

MAY 2010 LARGE PRINT TITLES

ROMANCE

Ruthless Magnate, Convenient Wife	Lynne Graham
The Prince's Chambermaid	Sharon Kendrick
The Virgin and His Majesty	Robyn Donald
Innocent Secretary...Accidentally Pregnant	Carol Marinelli
The Girl from Honeysuckle Farm	Jessica Steele
One Dance with the Cowboy	Donna Alward
The Daredevil Tycoon	Barbara McMahon
Hired: Sassy Assistant	Nina Harrington

HISTORICAL

Tall, Dark and Disreputable	Deb Marlowe
The Mistress of Hanover Square	Anne Herries
The Accidental Countess	Michelle Willingham

MEDICAL™

Country Midwife, Christmas Bride	Abigail Gordon
Greek Doctor: One Magical Christmas	Meredith Webber
Her Baby Out of the Blue	Alison Roberts
A Doctor, A Nurse: A Christmas Baby	Amy Andrews
Spanish Doctor, Pregnant Midwife	Anne Fraser
Expecting a Christmas Miracle	Laura Iding

millsandboon.co.uk Community

Join Us!

The Community is the perfect place to meet and chat to kindred spirits who love books and reading as much as you do, but it's also the place to:

- **Get the inside scoop from authors about their latest books**
- **Learn how to write a romance book with advice from our editors**
- **Help us to continue publishing the best in women's fiction**
- **Share your thoughts on the books we publish**
- **Befriend other users**

Forums: Interact with each other as well as authors, editors and a whole host of other users worldwide.

Blogs: Every registered community member has their own blog to tell the world what they're up to and what's on their mind.

Book Challenge: We're aiming to read 5,000 books and have joined forces with The Reading Agency in our inaugural Book Challenge.

Profile Page: Showcase yourself and keep a record of your recent community activity.

Social Networking: We've added buttons at the end of every post to share via digg, Facebook, Google, Yahoo, technorati and de.licio.us.

www.millsandboon.co.uk